ALSO BY KIMBERLY MULLINS:

Notebook Mysteries ~ Emma (Book 1)

Notebook Mysteries ~ Decisions and Possibilities (Book 2)

Notebook Mysteries ~ Changes and Challenges (Book 3)

Notebook Mysteries ~ Unexpected Outcomes (Book 4)

Notebook Mysteries ~ Haunted Christmas (a novella)

Notebook Mysteries ~ Suspicions (Book 5)

Notebook Mysteries ~ Parisian Intrigue (Book 6)

Notebook Mysteries ~ A Party to Remember (a novella)

Stand alone novels:

Divided Lives (K.R. Mullins)

1897 A Mark Sutherland Adventure

Notebook Mysteries

Notebook Mysteries

KIMBERLY MULLINS

NOTEBOOK MYSTERIES ~ Haunted Christmas

A novella in the Notebook Mysteries Series

Copyright © JKJ books, LLC 2022

First edition: September 2022

Mailing address for JKJ books, LLC; 17350 State Highway 249, STE 220 #3515 Houston, Texas 77064

Library of Congress Control Number: 2022905661

ISBN 979-8-9859930-3-5 (paperback)

ISBN 979-8-9859930-2-8 (ebook)

ISBN 979-8-9859930-5-9 (hardback)

This is a work of fiction. It is based on historical events within Chicago during the time period of the 1880s.

Edited by Kaitlyn Johnson, Strictly Textual

Cover Art by Miblart

To my dad who loved Christmas.
To Joshua and Jonathan, my loves always.

PROLOGUE

Clank, clank, clank. The sound of heavy chains seemed to be in concert with the pounding in his head.

He held his hands over his ears and huddled deeper into the bed. The clank of the chains could be heard again. "Marley?" he asked in a whisper and reached out a shaky hand to move the bed curtains back, revealing the dark room. "Marley?" he called again, louder this time.

The clanking seemed to be next to him. Startled, he pulled the curtains closed and sank back on the bed. "Go away, Marley, I don't want to see you."

A long, raspy moan could be heard in the room, and he tentatively stuck out his head again. He regretted it immediately and screamed as the apparition flew toward him.

"I need to get out!" He jumped out of the bed and ran to the balcony doors. "You won't get me!" he shouted as he jumped over the edge.

CHAPTER 1

A FEW WEEKS LATER

*E*mma pulled the paper out of her typewriter and placed it on her desk. She opened the drawer and pulled out the files needing to be updated. They were reviewed for any errors before being filed again. It was her last assignment from Mr. Pennington before the Christmas break.

Her position had started as a temporary one, but Mr. Pennington saw potential in her. In exchange for her investigations, he was teaching her how the law worked. The office would be closed after today for the holidays. *Christmas is approaching quickly; it's only five days away,* she thought.

The holiday was always busy for her family because of all the additional baking. In addition to her regular jobs, she was also helping out at Cousins, the family bakery.

A family party was held on Christmas Eve. Both boarding houses, family, and friends were invited to attend. Emma smiled. She was looking forward to the holidays.

She pulled out her bag to check her courier route for that day. It was open on her lap and she was reviewing the list of locations for document deliveries when a knock sounded on the door.

"Come in," she called absently.

Ethan Worthington, the law office secretary, stepped in. "Emma, you remember that favor you owe me?" he asked.

His tone was serious, and that got her full attention. She looked up and replied in a similar tone, "I do." Ethan had helped her on a previous case and, without him, the truth may not have been uncovered and a murderer might have gone free.

She put her bag aside and watched him as he paced her small office. He finally stopped in front of her. "I need you to investigate something for me, at my family home."

"Oh, if that's all, sure," she said, looking at him closely. She wondered why this request worried him so much.

"No, you don't understand. This house is haunted," he said desperately.

Emma looked at him in amazement. *Ethan is one of the more down-to-earth persons I know,* she thought. *This isn't something he's taking lightly.* She frowned at him. "Haunted? Ethan, what makes you say that?"

He looked around, not wanting anyone who might be in the office to overhear. "Can we meet after work and discuss this matter?"

She understood. He had responsibilities and couldn't take time out of his workday to review this with her. She pulled out her notebook. "When and what time would you like to meet?" she asked.

"Can I come to the boarding house this evening?" He knew her address from the files he kept on employees.

She thought ahead and asked, "Is 8:00pm too late?"

"No," he said, thinking quickly. "That's fine. I'll see you tonight."

He turned and left her office.

A haunted house? she thought. *This will be interesting.*

The clock bell chimed the hour. She looked toward it and thought, *Time is passing quickly.* Gathering her things, she dropped them into her bag. She hurriedly unbuttoned the long row of double buttons on her woolen skirt. It folded over, revealing a split skirt. The dashing design had been Dora's idea to help keep it from getting caught on her bike.

The bag was closed with a snap, and she made her way out to where Ethan's desk sat. Her winter things and her bike were stored in a nearby closet; she retrieved them before moving to the office entrance. Once there, she propped the bike against the door and pulled on her heavy coat, scarf, gloves, and hat. Bracing herself for the impact of the cold, she turned the knob to open the door.

Ethan found his sense of humor as he watched her prepare. He called, "Is that it? Any other layers to add?"

"It's cold out there today," she explained, turning back to him.

"Do you have courier work this afternoon?" he asked, frowning. The weather could be dangerous this time of year, and she normally stayed out all afternoon.

"A few engineering drawings to drop off," she confirmed. "I also told Cousin I would work an afternoon shift to get some orders caught up at the bakery."

"Be safe, don't take any unnecessary chances in this weather," he cautioned.

"I won't," she said as she took the bike by the handlebars to roll it outside onto the stoop. Once there, Emma tried to catch the breath the cold air had stolen from her. She opened her coat to let the air circulate some before buttoning it up again. The wind was brisk and would make her ride harder. The bike was lifted to her shoulder, she carried it down the stoop before jumping on it to go to her delivery locations.

Her teeth were chattering and her arms numb after finishing her deliveries. The thought of the warm bakery made her pedal harder to reach her final destination.

With a final push, she made it to the back door of the bakery.

She ducked her head down and pulled her bike toward the door. Grasping the door knob tightly, she pushed it and the wind tore it out of her hands, hitting the wall with a bang. A blast of hot air accompanied the yells from all parts of the bakery. "Shut the door!" she heard someone yell. Hurriedly, she placed the bike on her shoulder, grabbed the door handle, and leaned on it to push it closed. "I'm sorry," she called. There were some grumblings but most of the workers had a smile for Emma.

Cousin spotted her from his workstation and called out, "Thanks for helping out today." He indicated where she would work with his floured hand. "Your list is there," he told her.

"I'll get started as soon as I change," she said and made her way to the storage closet. She put her bike inside and stepped in to change into her bakery uniform. It was a white skirt with a white high-necked blouse and full sleeves. There was also an apron that buttoned on. Her work skirt had also been modified to a split style similar to the kind she wore when biking and was at least five inches shorter than that of the other female bakers.

She exited the room and made her way to her station, pulling on the baker's hat absently as she reviewed her list. The direction says the Apple cakes are to be cut into individual portions. *Not difficult,* she thought. *I just have to make a lot of them.*

She finished baking and moved the cakes from the baking trays to cool. The pastry boxes were lined up for her to fill. As they cooled, she cut them into squares and moved them into the boxes. *These will go out to the events scheduled for this evening,* she thought. The Christmas season had started, and there were parties almost every night.

"Will you be able to work the rest of the week?" asked Cousin as he approached her, his calendar out and pen at the ready.

"Yes, I can. Courier work is light right now."

He nodded, taking notes. "Good, good. Once you get those

boxed up you may head out for today. What time can we plan on you being here tomorrow?"

"Let's say early afternoon, for three hours. I have some activities that will probably take up my morning," she said, thinking about her meeting with Ethan that night. *There may be some follow-up to take care of.*

Cousin marked it down and headed back to his office.

Emma cleaned up her workstation and made her way to the closet to change clothes. She called goodbye to the other bakers as she walked her bike out.

It wasn't quite dark when she left, but it would be by the time she got home. She pushed herself to get there as soon as possible. There seemed to be something sinister in the cold that evening.

CHAPTER 2

*D*inner had been served and the dishes were removed from the boarding house dining room. The remaining people at the table were Tim, Dora, Emma, Jeremy, and Jake. Savannah had a play that would have her getting in late. Jake was preoccupied with a new book he had gotten. It was by Edward M. Estabrook, *Photography in the Studio and in the Field.* His interest in photography had expanded to reading books about new developing technologies.

"Tell us who's coming over tonight and why," Dora demanded. Emma had commented when she got home that there would be a visitor that evening.

"Ethan Worthington, the secretary at Mr. Pennington's office, has a favor to ask," Emma explained.

"Do you have any idea what the favor entails?" asked Jeremy, settling back in his chair with his coffee cup in his hands.

"Yes," she said. She wasn't sure how to tell the group what Ethan wanted her to investigate.

"And?" Tim asked, prompting her.

Emma looked at him and said reluctantly, "He says his family home is haunted."

They looked at her, astonished.

"Haunted? You mean spirits?" Dora asked.

"Or ghosts?" suggested Jeremy.

"Is he serious?" Dora asked. She didn't believe someone would ask Emma for something like this.

"Something has put this notion in his head. He's coming over tonight to review the case with us. He'll be here at eight. I think we should hear him out and take him seriously. I don't want him to feel we are making fun of him," Emma warned.

Dora said immediately, "No, we wouldn't do that."

Tim and Jeremy agreed.

"Emma," Jake spoke up, sounding nervous. "Are there really ghosts in that house?"

She reached over to touch his arm. "Jake, there hasn't been any scientific or photographic evidence to suggest they exist."

He nodded, understanding. "Then why are we going to check into it? To show him they aren't real?"

"That's it exactly. But we will listen politely to what he has to say," Emma stated.

"Yes, we will," he confirmed and lowered his head to read from his book.

Dora stood up. "I need to check on Lottie." She looked over at Tim. "Check on Patrick and see if he's ready to be read to."

Tim reached over to take her hand and accompanied her upstairs. They separated at their bedroom door. She entered her bedroom and walked toward the curtain in her room. Since Lottie had been born, they had added a temporary curtain wall to separate their room from hers, to allow them some privacy while she slept. It would be a while yet before she got her own room. Tim headed next door to Patrick. He pushed the door open and found him sitting up holding a book. "Waiting for me?" he asked. Patrick grinned and scooted over so he could join him on the bed.

After the kids were all settled, Tim and Dora rejoined Emma

and Jeremy, and Jake in the sitting room, talking and waiting for
Ethan to arrive.

CHAPTER 3

s the clock chimed 8:00, they heard a knock at the door. Emma put down her book and got up. "He's on time. I'll get it."

She entered the foyer and approached the door. The knock sounded again as she went to open it. Ethan stood in the doorway, wringing his hat like a wet rag. *He's normally so self-assured,* she thought. She looked at him closely. "Won't you come in?" she asked.

He started to enter but stopped abruptly, "Emma, I appreciate you taking this seriously."

"We want to help you," she assured him. "But I want more details before I agree to anything."

"Of course," he said, taking a deep breath to calm himself.

"Would you mind coming into the sitting room? The people here are part of my team," she said, hoping to get him moving.

He walked in slowly and looked at her as she shut the door. "Team?" he asked, his voice sounding hoarse as he started twisting his hat again.

"Would you like me to take your coat and hat?" she asked kindly.

He looked down at it before he handed it over to her. "I'm not sure it could still be called a hat," he said, his mouth twisted into a humorless smile as he shrugged out of his coat.

She didn't comment as she took the garment and laid them on the small table near them. "Are you ready to go in?"

"There'll be more people who know about this?" he asked, twisting his hands he wished he hadn't relinquished his hat.

"Yes, for my cases, it's usually more than just me," she explained, frowning as she continued to observe him.

"Oh, of course. I should have realized," he muttered. He had heard about the many cases Emma worked on and, given their complexity, he shouldn't have been surprised that there were more people involved.

"This way," she said as she guided him to the sitting room. He hesitated at the doorway, his eyes darting to each new face.

"Let me introduce you," Emma said softly, trying to settle him in. "Everyone, this is Ethan Worthington. Ethan, this is my team: Tim Flannigan, my brother-in-law; Dora, his wife, and my sister; and Jeremy Tilden, my close friend," she said with a wink and a smile. She continued, "Jake is our friend and photographer."

"It's nice to meet you all," Ethan said awkwardly.

"Why don't you take a seat?" inquired Dora.

"That would be nice, thank you."

He walked over and sat on the settee; Emma joined him there.

"Ethan, why don't you tell everyone about you first."

He looked around the room. "Well, I work with Emma as Mr. Pennington's secretary. I've held the position for the past five years."

"We understand you need some help," Jeremy stated, hoping to steer the man to reveal the favor.

"Yes. I've inherited my family home. My father passed away a few weeks ago," he said, dropping his head in his hands.

"Ethan, I didn't know..." Emma said, reaching out to touch his arm.

"We are so sorry," Dora commented for the group.

"Thank you," said Ethan sincerely, removing his hands from his face.

"Was it unexpected?" Emma asked as she drew back her hand, trying to approach him slowly.

"Yes." Ethan took a breath to steady himself before continuing. "The police say he jumped off the balcony located just off his bedroom." He leaned forward earnestly. "I just don't think he would have jumped on his own. There is something in that house that made him do it."

"Did your father have any medical problems?" Emma probed.

"No, not that I know of. I had dinner with him once a week and he never said anything was wrong."

"Did he have a personal physician?" asked Emma.

"Yes, Dr. Warner. He's here in town. I can provide you with his address."

"Thank you," Emma said and wrote the information he provided in her notebook.

"Ethan," asked Jeremy, "did your father drink alcohol?"

He shook his head. "No, he never did. He just didn't feel it was necessary."

"Did he exhibit any signs of depression?" Dora asked. She was thinking about the suicide determination.

"No. In fact, he was planning a big Christmas celebration. Does a man making plans like that kill himself?"

"I wouldn't think so," commented Tim.

"Was he seeing anyone, socially?" Jeremy asked.

"No, not that I'm aware of. He didn't want to date after Mom passed," Ethan stated.

"Were there any witnesses? Household staff?" Emma asked.

"We can't keep them. The ones who were there had only

been employed a few weeks, but they had run off the day before. The only staff to stay was Mrs. Shephard. She and her son have always been with us."

"What do Mrs. Shephard and her son do for you?" asked Tim.

"Housekeeping and carriage driver. The other staff members were a cook and two maids."

"Did the police question them?" asked Emma.

"I believed they planned to, but since it was ruled a suicide, they didn't follow through."

"I can check on that," Emma commented. "What's the detective's name?"

"Detective Kelly."

Emma noted that fact and looked at Jake thoughtfully, wondering if he had photos of the crime scene. She made a note to follow up with him. Jake would want her to follow protocol when she asked for them.

"You said you had trouble keeping staff. Why won't they stay?" Tim asked curiously. He, Dora, and Emma ran a temporary employment agency, and keeping employees was important.

"They believe the house is haunted. They've complained that they hear and see things, especially at night," explained Ethan.

Jeremy was curious. "Can you describe some of these?"

"At night, you can hear footsteps walking down the halls when no one is there. Windows rattle and knobs turn by themselves. Creaks and moans that can't be explained."

Emma frowned. "How old is the home?"

"More than fifty years old. My grandfather was a carpenter and stone mason. The final design is based on the gothic style. My father continued to work on the house after his dad's death."

"Did you work on it also?" asked Dora.

He looked down at his hands and said, "No. I'm not great with tools. I do better in the business world."

"Ethan," Emma said, "older homes will tend to move with age and the footsteps could be the floors cooling off at night."

"Yes," he agreed. "The house has always had those sounds. As a boy, I would stay up listening for the steps down the hallway before I went to sleep." He paused a moment and said, "If that was the only thing, then I wouldn't have come to see you."

The group sat forward in their chairs collectively, waiting.

"It's my father's room. In the past month, the staff has refused to clean it. We had reports from different maids that they witnessed apparitions there."

"What kind of apparitions?" asked Dora, her voice higher than normal.

"They don't seem to be consistent. I questioned them, but there were no common factors."

Emma looked at Ethan. "Where is the house located?"

"It is north of the main city."

"Did your father always live there, full time?" asked Tim.

"Not since my mom died. He moved to an apartment near mine. We were very close," he said, his mouth drawing down and his eyes dropping.

Dora watched and felt so sad for the man who was now so alone.

"Did your father report seeing any of the apparitions?" Tim asked curiously.

"No," Ethan answered simply.

"How long has it been since you have stayed in the house?" Jeremy asked.

"Last Christmas," Ethan answered, trying to pull himself out of his depressed state.

"Why is that?" Emma asked.

"It's our tradition to stay there over the holiday and have dinner," he explained. "Father had moved back in to get the house organized for the holiday. He wanted a deep cleaning of all of the rooms and wanted to oversee the installation of Christmas decorations."

So, the timeline for this starts just before Christmas this year, thought Emma. "You haven't been there since that time?" she asked

"No, I haven't had a reason to be there."

Emma asked the hard question. "Ethan, why do you think he didn't kill himself?"

The man's face turned ashen at the question, and he replied in a low voice, full of pain. "He wouldn't have done that. He loved his life and would never take it. I know he was killed. Either by a ghost or someone else in the house. Could you look into it for me, *please?*"

Emma looked at him closely before saying, "We will look into it."

Color flooded into Ethan's face and he looked hopeful for the first time that night.

Emma studied her notes. "The house, who owns it now?"

"I do," he said simply. "I'm the last of the family."

"Your father had no brothers or sisters?" Dora asked.

"Well, I did have an uncle, but he died before I was born. I'll be making the ownership official in a probate hearing tomorrow." He noticed the time. "I'm sorry I kept you up so late," he said apologetically.

Just as Emma was about to reply, they heard the front door open and close with a bang. *Savannah,* she thought. That was confirmed when the woman strolled into the sitting room. She wore dark clothes and looked more like a burglar than someone who worked at the theatre. The dark clothes allowed her to move around the set, getting it ready for approaching scenes.

"Hey, the play went well tonight..." She noticed they had a guest and stopped what she was saying.

Emma waved her over. "Ethan this is Savannah Woods. She works as a stage manager at a local theatre and also serves as a member of our team." She looked over at Savannah and continued. "Savannah, Ethan stopped by to talk to us about a case we are taking on."

"It's nice to meet you, Ethan." She looked back at Emma. "You can catch me up tomorrow. I'm going to head up to bed now; it was a long night at the theatre."

Ethan watched her leave the room, somewhat bemused at the sudden appearance and then disappearance of the lovely girl.

Emma saw his attention was elsewhere. "Ethan?" she prompted him,

He dragged his gaze away from the door and said, "Huh? Oh, Yes."

She closed her notebook with a snap. "Why don't we end this here and I'll come by tomorrow morning to review the next steps with you."

"Oh, okay, great," he said absently, still watching the door where Savannah had exited.

Emma smiled slightly and stood, with Ethan following her to the foyer. She got his coat and hat, which he took from her gratefully and walked him to the front door. He slid the coat on and placed his hat on his head.

She laughed suddenly. Covering her mouth quickly with her hand, she said, "I think you need a new hat."

He removed it and turned it over in his hands, commenting wryly, "I think you're right." He stopped and suddenly grabbed her elbow. "Thank you for listening to me and helping me with this matter."

"Don't worry, we'll look into this," she assured him.

With that, he exited into the night, his fists tightly clinched in his pockets.

Emma closed the door behind Ethan and leaned against it.

CHAPTER 4

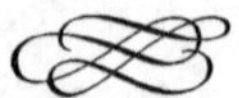

When Emma didn't return, Jeremy went out into the foyer to find her. He saw her leaning on the door.

"What are you thinking?" he asked, watching her drum her fingers on her lips. He knew she was thinking deeply about the case when he saw her doing that.

"Let's go back to the sitting room," she suggested as she lowered her hand to take his.

They walked back into the sitting room and sat down. She pulled out her notebook and said, "Okay, let's go over the examples of haunting he mentioned one by one. First, the windows rattling."

"That could be wind and loose windows," Tim commented.

Emma looked at her list. "Second, footsteps walking the halls at night; could be just the heat cooling off of the floors at the end of the day."

"What else?" Dora asked, fascinated.

"Doorknobs turning at night when people are in bed."

"Explainable as pranksters or an active imagination. Especially in a large, mostly empty house," said Jeremy thoughtfully.

"It might just be the poor man died and Ethan can't accept it," suggested Dora.

"Jake," Emma said suddenly. He looked up from his book at her. He had stayed in the room but remained quiet during the discussion with Ethan.

"Yes?"

"Were you on the scene when they found Mr. Worthington's body?"

"I was called in to take the photos," he confirmed.

Good, thought Emma. "I'd like to see them."

"You will have to get approval first from the detective in charge of the case."

She expected that response and nodded. "I understand, and I'll get the approval and come see you at the station."

"Tomorrow?"

"If I can work it out."

Tim looked at the group. "So, we are taking a case involving a ghost?"

"Yes. I owe Ethan and would like to do this for him," Emma explained. "Additionally, how fun would it be to investigate a ghost during the Christmas season? It has a very Dickensian feel to it," she said, referencing the 1843 book *A Christmas Carol.*

Jeremy smiled slightly. "Where do we go from here?"

"First, I need to get a copy of that police report and then talk to the doctor. We need to know the listed cause of death."

"What about the servants?" asked Dora. Getting information from servants had helped in several of their other cases.

"We need to find them," Emma confirmed. "I'll get a list from Ethan tomorrow and see if you or Amy know them."

"Agreed," Dora said, yawning broadly.

Seeing her yawn and noticing the hour, Tim said, "It's late, let's get to bed. We can pick this up in the morning."

Everyone agreed. Jeremy, Tim, and Jake worked to turn off the gas lamps as Dora and Emma headed upstairs.

CHAPTER 5

The next morning, Emma and Jeremy were getting dressed in Emma's room.

"Where are you headed this morning?" he asked.

She looked over at him as she slipped on her long jacket. "Police station first, then over to Mr. Pennington's office to see Ethan."

"I thought the office was closed until after the holidays."

"It is," she confirmed, "but Ethan is there closing some cases for the year-end. He also mentioned his father's probate hearing is today. I want to see if I can accompany him. I'd like to see how the process works." She pulled out her notebook. "The rest of the morning, I plan to follow up with the doctor and a few others."

They finished dressing. Jeremy walked into his room and then they walked out of their respective bedrooms and met in the hallway to make their way downstairs for breakfast.

"What will you be doing today?" she asked.

"Not much. It's slow so we'll be straightening up and closing files for the year. We'll also be looking at the caseloads for next year."

As they entered the dining room, they saw Dora sitting at the table with baby Lottie, feeding her breakfast. Dora looked up as they entered. "Set the table, please."

"And good morning to you also," teased Emma, kissing her on her head. She leaned over and gave one to Lottie also. The little girl squealed and grabbed at her hair. "Mama says I have to help set the table," Emma said as she disengaged the child's fingers and moved over to the sideboard where she started pulling out napkins and silverware. Jeremy gathered the plates and carried them over to the table to distribute them.

Amy came into the room at that moment and rang the breakfast bell, located near the dining-room door. Patrick, Dora and Tim's adopted son, came running in and wrapped his arms around Emma's legs in a big hug.

"Good morning, Patrick," she commented as she tried to stay upright.

"Good morning, Emma," he said brightly, tilting his face toward hers, revealing a wide smile.

"Morning, Tim," Emma said as her brother-in-law walked in at a slower pace behind Patrick.

"Patrick, try not to knock down your aunt," the boy's father scolded lightly.

"He's fine," Emma assured him, hugging the boy tightly.

"Emma, I need you to stick around after breakfast to review current jobs."

Tim, Dora, and Emma had been running a temporary employment business for the last six years. It required all three of them to have input into the positions and people available. Emma participated as a co-owner and as an employee of their business.

"That shouldn't be a problem. I have time." She knew the police officers she wanted to speak with wouldn't be at the precinct for another hour. Looking around she asked, "Where is Jake?"

Ethyl answered, "A note came early this morning, he had to go to a crime scene to take pictures." She and Jake had developed a close friendship since she started working at the boarding house.

"Oh, I had hoped to go in with him," Emma said.

"I need help with the trays, please," Amy interrupted her thought and called out from the kitchen door. Her assistant Ethyl picked up the pitchers she had filled and moved them to the dining room.

Everyone got up to bring the food to the table. Dora stayed with the kids.

Breakfast went quickly; the food was always amazing. Emma was concentrating on her plans for the day and let the conversation flow around her.

After breakfast was cleared away, Jeremy leaned over and kissed her. "I have to head in to work a little early this morning. Try to check in with me later, if you can."

"I will," she promised. "I'll be at the bakery in the afternoon today."

"Bring back something sweet?" he asked hopefully.

"I think I can manage that for you."

"Love you," he commented softly.

"Love you, too," she said in the same tone and watched him leave.

Tim cleared his throat. "Ready to start?" He had his books set out.

"Let me get Lottie cleaned up and changed. Can you give me a minute?" Dora asked.

"Of course."

Dora took the baby and headed out of the room.

"Papa?" Patrick got up from his chair and stood by Tim.

"Yes?" Tim asked, giving him his full attention.

"Grandpapa said I could work with him at his house this afternoon if you can take me."

Tim pretended to think about it. "I think I can work that out. Do you want to start your homework soon?"

"Can I start at nine?" the boy negotiated.

Tim smiled and ruffled his thick red hair. "That would be fine. What are you going to do now?"

"I want to go over to Tommy's house. May I go?" Patrick knew he needed permission before going out. Tommy was the grandson of Dora and Emma's Uncle Hans, and he was visiting for the holidays. Their house was only a few doors down from the boarding house.

"Yes, but you must get bundled up and you must pass inspection with your mama. Understood?"

"Yes, Papa," Patrick said before running out of the room to get his coat and a ball.

"Don't forget your hat, gloves, and scarf!" Tim called after him.

"I won't," the boy called back.

Dora came back downstairs, carrying a cleaned-up Lottie. She heard the conversation between Patrick and Tim. "Where's Patrick going?"

"Next door to see Tommy, maybe play some ball. He'll see you before he leaves," Tim said, knowing his wife was protective of him.

Dora looked satisfied with that comment and set Lottie down on the floor next to her chair with her toy blocks. She walked over to the sideboard, pulled out her accounting books, and moved back to the table.

When Lottie started to crawl under the table, Dora called out, "Amy!"

The other woman stuck her head through the door to the kitchen. "Yes, Dora?"

"Could you watch Lottie during our meeting?"

Amy smiled broadly, always enjoying her time with the baby. "Of course." She bent down to look at Lottie under the table.

"Come here, baby girl." Lottie crawled quickly to her. She picked up the girl and they went back into the kitchen.

Patrick raced in dressed in his winter gear to stand in front of his mama. "Mama, am I warm enough?"

Dora looked him over and, as she wrapped his scarf more tightly around his neck, said in a serious voice said, "You may not be outside without your hat and scarf on."

He looked down when she made that comment.

"Patrick," she said, taking his chin in her hands and forcing him to look her in the eyes.

"Yes, Mama, but sometimes I get hot with all of this on. Especially if we're playing ball."

She thought about that. "Okay, you may unbutton your jacket for some airflow, but no rolling around in the wet snow. Understood?"

"Yes, Mama," he said respectfully.

"On your way now," she said, letting him go.

Tim watched as Patrick ran off and called after him, "Don't forget your ball. And come back at nine."

"Yes, Papa," he called back.

"I'll come to get you if you forget," Tim warned.

"Yes, Papa."

They heard the front door slam behind him.

"It's been nice with Tommy visiting," Tim said.

"Yes, and more of his cousins will be here closer to Christmas," Dora commented.

"The party is going to be big this year," Emma said, looking forward to it.

"We'll need temporary help to help prepare and serve," Dora reminded him.

Tim looked at his notes. "I'll give you a list of people we have available, so you can choose who you'd like to help out."

"And we'll need to get at least three trees," Dora commented, thinking ahead to the party.

"Patrick and I can go this morning and pick them out. What night do we want to decorate?" asked Tim.

"I think soon; we don't want to wait until the party." She looked over at Emma. "If we get organized, can you help tonight?"

"I don't think Jeremy has any plans, and I'm free," Emma said.

"Good," Dora said decisively. "We'll include Savannah and Jake also."

"Don't forget Abbey, Papa, and Cole," reminded Emma.

Dora nodded. "Yes, of course. I'll send them a note this morning. I hope it isn't too short notice."

"It should be fine. I think the weather is limiting any plans right now," said Emma.

"Do you want me to start pulling out the Christmas decoration boxes this morning?" Tim asked

"Yes, please," Dora said.

"Patrick will be excited, and Lottie will be more aware of the holiday this year," Emma said.

"Oh, dear. We'll have to keep Lottie away from the trees." The baby hadn't been mobile last Christmas, so the concern wasn't there.

"Probably no candles this year," Emma said thoughtfully. Their trees were normally lit with them. She enjoyed the tradition, but it could be a fire hazard, especially with a little one.

"Definitely not," her sister said, picturing what would happen if Lottie pulled down a fully lit tree.

"Agreed," said Tim.

Emma looked around the room, imagining the decorations in place. There would be Christmas wreaths, wood railings festooned with evergreens, and cotton batting for snow. "It all sounds lovely. Do you want me to bring home some sweets to have as we're decorating?"

"That would be nice. I'd rather not spring this on Amy," Dora said. "I'll pop popcorn for the children to string." *And,* she thought, *I'll also make popcorn balls.* Other decorations would include stars cut from gilt paper and lace bags filled with bright candies that would be fastened to the tree's branches.

"And candies strung with the popcorn?" Emma asked.

"Yes, and candies will be strung with them," Dora confirmed, knowing how much Emma enjoyed that tradition.

"I'll also bring some decorative cookies to hang on the trees," Emma promised.

Dora glanced over at Tim; she could see he was getting impatient to start the meeting.

"Ready?" Tim asked with a slight smile.

"Yes," they both commented in a business-like tone.

"We have a larger than normal contingent of employees at the department stores because of Christmas. They've all been notified of their last days. A few stores, along with Marshall Fields and Stubings, have commented that they'd like the employees to stay an extra week after Christmas to do an inventory check."

"Is everyone still available?" asked Dora.

"They should be. I'm hoping we'll have five of the women out of the group apply for business school in the spring." The Carlyle Charity, where they were board members, continued to support women's education. It also helped their business to have more qualified women to work in the engineering offices.

"Has Claire been notified, in case financial support is needed?" Emma asked. Clair Spencer headed the charity and distributed funds to the organizations or people in need.

"I've told her the number, but I need to confirm the names," he commented, taking notes.

"Great."

"Emma, how's the work at Mr. Pennington's office going? Do we need to start training someone to replace you?" Tim asked, looking down at his notes.

"No, I really like it there, and I think Mr. Pennington would like me to work more permanently. We may think about adding a clerk in the future when I'm doing less office work and more investigations."

"We can work on that," he said, making a note in his books. "Outside jobs are almost nonexistent right now due to the snow."

"Do we have enough inside construction going on to keep those employees busy?" asked Dora. She was concerned that the workers would not have paychecks during the holiday season.

"Yes, a lot of the jobs thought ahead and made sure that the finishing work was going on inside. We shouldn't have to lay anyone off. Any other issues?" He looked at Emma and Dora. They shook their heads. "No? Okay, then." He closed his books and stood up to return to the study.

"I need to be on my way," Emma said, heading to the foyer closet.

Dora followed and watched her bundle up. Emma looked over at her and teased, "Do you want to inspect me also?"

Dora took her seriously, walked over to her, picked up her muffler, and wrapped it around her neck. She looked at her sister and asked, "Pants today?" It was unsafe to be out in the weather without pants and long underwear.

"Definitely during the winter months," Emma said, picking up her bag and placing her winter hat on her head. Her bakery clothes were in her bag for her afternoon job.

Dora reached up and straightened it, tucking in Emma's braid. "Yes, I think you're okay now," she stated as she finished her inspection.

Emma smiled, leaned over, and kissed her. "Have a great day."

She made her way through the kitchen, pausing to give Lottie a big kiss. She sidled out the door as she told Ethyl and Amy goodbye.

Dora called to Tim, "Don't forget we'll need three trees by tonight."

"I want to wait for Patrick so he can go with me," he called back.

Dora looked out the window, letting her forehead rest on the cold glass. The snow didn't look like it was going to abate anytime soon, and she worried about her family being out in it.

CHAPTER 6

*E*mma rode over to the police station on her bicycle. *Ghosts, Ethan's father, maids running away…she thought. What is going on in that house?*

Sleet rained down her face, and she burrowed further into her muffler. The precinct was close. She increased her pedaling speed, thinking only of getting out of the cold.

Her front wheel hit an ice patch, causing the bike to swerve to the right and hit a large rock. She flew over the handlebars, quickly rolled herself into a ball, and fell into the snow. *I'm going to be in trouble with Dora,* she thought as she lay there. *I'm not supposed to be rolling around in the snow.*

Sitting up, she wiped the snow off her head and shoulders and checked for injuries. The many layers had offered additional protection, so no harm was done. Relieved, she got to her feet, walked over to her bike, pulled it out of the snow, and examined it. The front wheel was damaged. She'd have to carry it the rest of the way to the station. *It's my own fault,* she thought. *I was going too fast on icy streets.* She placed the bike on her shoulder and trudged through the snow to the police station.

Emma kept it with her as she made her way up the stoop and

into the station. As she entered, she closed the door quickly behind her, looking around the open entryway. Brushing the sleet off her forehead, she unwrapped her scarf and set her bike down on the tile floor.

The desk clerk, Officer Jessup, watched her walk over to him, dragging the bike with her. He looked at her from his tall desk and said in a cheerful voice, "Hello, Emma. What are you doing out in this cold weather?"

"I stopped by to check on something." She pulled out her notebook. "Is Detective John Kelly here? He is working the Worthington case."

Jessup looked down at his logbook. "Yes, he's here. Third floor. Is he expecting you?"

"No, I got his name from Ethan Worthington. He asked me to look into his father's death."

"It should be okay." The officer knew Emma was friends with the police chief and would be allowed to go up unescorted. "Just ask for him on the third floor."

"I will," she said. She looked down at the damaged bike and back up at the desk officer. "Would it be all right if I leave this here?"

He looked over his desk and down at it. "It looks like it's been through the wars. Sure, roll it behind here. I'll keep an eye on it."

"Well, it doesn't roll anymore."

He gave it a considering look as she dragged it behind his desk.

"Thanks," she said and headed up the three flights of stairs. The door was opened revealing a room full of desks and people. At the first one, she stopped and asked the young detective sitting there, "Can you direct me to Detective Kelly?"

He cocked his head to the right. "Over there."

She looked to where he indicated and saw a tall, thin man standing in front of the desk moving papers and folders around.

She took in his appearance; he had blondish-brown hair and appeared to be in his early thirties.

"Thank you," she said and headed over to him. As she got close, she asked, "Detective Kelly?"

He turned toward her and asked, "Yes, and you would be?"

"Emma Evans."

John Kelly realized he knew that name. He sat on the edge of his desk and folded his arms. "I've heard of you," he said.

Emma was unsure how to take that comment. "I wanted to speak with you about a case you are involved in, Detective."

"Call me John, and that depends on the case you want to talk about, Miss Evans."

"Call me Emma," she responded.

Kelly stood up and moved around the desk to his chair. "Why don't you sit down and tell me what this is about?"

She sat in the chair in front of his desk, then pulled out her notebook. "Louis Worthington. As I understand it, he jumped off his balcony at his property in upper Chicago."

"Let me check. That one was just here." Kelly moved some files around and pulled one out. He opened it, scanning the information.

Emma noticed the size of the file. "Rather thin," she commented.

"Yes," he said absently. "There wasn't a lot to that one. It was clear that it was a suicide."

"Can you tell me about it?"

"Can I ask why the interest?" he asked, looking over at her before sharing.

"His son asked me to look into it. He's concerned there's more to it. He doesn't believe it was a suicide."

"The son. His name is Ethan?"

She nodded.

"Yes, I got that impression from him at the scene and in later interviews with him."

"Can you tell me the details of the case and how you determined it was a suicide?"

He gave her a long look, then glanced down at the file. "We were notified that a body was found at the Worthington house."

"Who found him?"

"It was a delivery person, a young man by the name of Richard Wilkins. He had an early morning delivery."

"Did you get to talk to him?"

"I did. He came straight here to report it and rode back with us."

"What did you find when you got there?"

"The body, lying just as he said," Kelly confirmed.

"What was your first impression?"

"Initially, it appeared to be an accident. It looked like Worthington had fallen off the balcony and hit his head on a rock."

"Appeared?" she questioned.

He looked back at his notes. "We went into the house and to the bedroom. The balcony door's latch was broken and the doors were wide open to the outside. When we went out there, we saw the railing was high—too high to just fall off. We also found a chair on the balcony right at the railing. It was in just the right place to climb onto and jump off."

"So, you changed the focus of your investigation to a suicide," she stated.

"Yes," he said simply.

"Did a doctor take a look at the body?"

"Yes. We notified his personal physician to examine it and confirm our findings."

"Did Jake take any pictures at the scene?" she asked, drumming her fingers on her lips.

He looked through the file again. "Yes, they're here. Are you sure you'd like to view them?"

"I'll be fine," she assured him as she held out her hand.

John handed them to her. She looked at each one, examining the body's position.

"What did the doctor say after he reviewed these?" Emma asked.

"He confirmed that Mr. Worthington fell and his head hit the rock. It was probably what killed him. He can't confirm if he jumped or was made to jump. The only thing he could positively confirm was that he'd fallen, hit his head, and died."

"Did he say anything else?" she inquired, studying the photos.

"No."

"Hmm," she said, thinking that the arms looked fractured. *If he was going to kill himself, would he have this kind of injury?* When she fell off her bike today, her instinct had been to put out her arms, but her training told her to roll herself into a ball before hitting the ground. "I'll follow up with the doctor." She continued her questions. "Did you interview the staff?"

"We had planned to initially, but when the death appeared to be a suicide, there didn't seem to be a reason. It was also hard to locate all of them. Several had run off a few days before. It was reported that they were scared of something."

"Did you find out what scared them?"

He looked a bit embarrassed. "As we understand from the agency that placed them, they believe the house was haunted."

Emma didn't say anything about his comment and asked, "Were there additional pictures of the scene?" She hadn't seen any others in the packet.

"Jake has them. I took the ones that showed the victim for the case file."

"Would you mind if I get a copy of these and the ones showing the house?"

"We can arrange that with Jake." He opened a drawer, pulled out a form, and filled it out. He handed it to her. "Just give this to him."

"Thank you. What about the staff, do you have their names?" she added, thinking that she needed to follow up with them.

"I don't, we didn't need them at the time. Also, Ethan mentioned that two people work there permanently."

"Yes, I have their names. Where were they when Mr. Worthington died?"

He looked at the file and back at her. "Ethan mentioned they were off that evening."

"Hmm," she said. "I'll interview them also."

"Emma," he said firmly. "You need to let me know if anything changes on the case. I don't want to be surprised."

"I will," she promised. She gathered up her things and stood. "Thank you for your time." She took a few steps and turned toward him, "Jake went out to a crime scene this morning..."

"Actually two," he confirmed.

"Would you mind if I take a look at the pictures from these scenes?"

He frowned and ask, "Why?"

"Call it curiosity for now."

"It is Detective Carlson's case, but he shouldn't have a problem with you just viewing them. Hand me the form," he requested.

She handed it to him and he amended it to allow her to view the other scene's pictures. The paper was returned to her and she headed back out the way she came.

He nodded and watched her with a contemplative look on his face.

Taking the stairs two at a time, she exited quickly into the main entrance. Officer Jessup was still at his desk, she headed toward him.

He heard boots clinking on the tile floors, he looked and saw Emma. "Get what you needed?"

"I did. Thanks for the help. Would you mind hanging on to

my bike for a few more minutes? I want to see Jake before I leave."

"Go ahead, I'm not leaving the area anytime soon."

She smiled at him and turned to make her way to Jake's lab, located in the basement of the police station. Gas lamps lit her way down to the area he used to develop his film.

"Jake," she called. She heard an immediate reply

"I am developing pictures, please wait."

The development process could take some time, so she sat in a nearby chair and pulled out her notebook to review the details of the case.

It was a few minutes later when he opened the door to his lab. "You can come in now."

She walked in, looking around, curious as to what his new case was. He had pictures hung on a wire above his counter to dry.

He pulled her out of her observations by asking brusquely, "What can I help you with?"

"Detective Kelly said I could pick up the pictures from a case."

"Do you have approval?" He was ready to turn her down if she didn't follow the procedure.

She smiled at him slightly. "Of course." Emma handed him the form. "Kelly also said I could view the ones from this morning."

He reviewed the note thoroughly and nodded. "Let me get this for you. The ones from this morning are there," he pointed to the wire holding the pictures.

As he went to get the items she requested, she studied the drying pictures. "Kelly mentioned that there were two scenes?"

"Yes, two separate ones. We just got back from the second scene," he said, looking at the pictures she'd referenced.

"These are very similar. You said they were two different cases?" She reviewed each one closely.

"Yes."

"When were they found?"

"Both were reported this morning. I was going to develop the film from the first one, but I got called to go to the second scene before I could process them."

"Kelly mentioned this is Detective Carlson's case."

"Yes."

She continued looking closely at the pictures.

"Did you want to review these before you leave?" he asked, pulling out the requested pictures from the Worthington crime scene file.

"If you have time…"

"I do." He made room for her to lay the pictures on his bench. She spread them out.

"Are we still investigating the ghost?"

"Well," she quantified, "we're investigating what happened to Mr. Worthington."

He nodded. "What did you want to review with me?"

She pointed to the picture of the victim's head. "I understand the cause of death was his head hitting a rock."

"Yes," Jake confirmed. "I have a picture of the rock and the wound inflicted." He moved the pictures closer for her review.

She looked closely at them. "That's not a rock that could be moved easily." It was partially buried in the ground. She looked over at him and asked, "Did you go inside?"

"I did."

"Did you take pictures of the room?"

"It is part of the scene," he commented, moving more pictures closer to her.

She studied the room and the balcony carefully. *Smart,* she thought as she noticed Jake had Detective Kelly stand by the balcony to give perspective to the pictures. It was formed out of heavy wood and was over four feet in height. "Going under would have been impossible," she commented.

Jake understood what she was talking about. "The railings were very close together. Going through them would have made that difficult."

It's also too tall, she thought, noting Detective Kelly's height. *The detective was right, it wouldn't have been easy to get over without assistance.* She noticed something in the corner of the picture. "What's that object?" she asked, pointing at it.

He handed her another picture and said, "This one is a better picture." It showed a chair sitting at the balcony rail.

"Detective Kelly mentioned that," she murmured. "Was it in that position when you got there?"

"We didn't move anything; the scene is exactly as you see it."

"Do we think the chair was placed there so he could jump off the balcony?"

Jake had no opinion. He liked to present his data and let police officers make the determination.

Studying the body again, she reexamined the injuries. *The doctor,* she thought. *I need to talk to him.* She gathered all of them up, placed them in an envelope, and slipped them into her bag. Something was bothering her; she glanced at the still drying pictures again. "These are very similar," she said again, studying each one intently.

"Possibly, but that is up to the detective and not me."

"See these marks here?" she asked, indicating the first girl's neck.

He looked over. "Yes."

"And look at the marks on the second girl's neck. Whatever was used to strangle the first one was also used to strangle the second one. These are very distinctive; they appear to have twisted the weapon during the attack."

Jake looked closer, studying the pattern. "Probably some type of rope, and it looks like it was twisted similarly."

"Will you tell the detective?" she asked.

"I will add it to my report when I turn in the pictures."

"Okay, thanks for reviewing these with me," she said, patting her bag that held the envelope.

He nodded and started working on his report.

"Jake." She waited for him to look up. "We're going to decorate the house tonight."

"I will be there on time."

"I expected that," she said with a smile and headed back upstairs. As she ascended, she thought about the information she'd learned. So far, there was no evidence that Ethan's father had been murdered. Just some odd stories about that house and the supposed haunting.

CHAPTER 7

$\mathcal{E}$mma exited the basement and headed to the desk where she had left her bike. She looked around and didn't see Officer Jessup or the bike. Frowning, she studied the area as she slipped on her coat and hat.

"Looking for something?" a voice called from behind her.

She turned around and saw the officer rolling her bike in from outside.

She ran over and knelt, checking the tire. "You fixed it! I damaged it when I fell."

"Sure. It was easy. The front fender was bent against the wheel. I just hammered it out and it's good as new."

She stood up and said gratefully, "Thanks so much for doing that."

"No problem, did you get what you needed from Kelly?"

"I did," she said as she rolled the bike back and forth. She grinned at him and said, "Thanks again, and Merry Christmas!"

"You too!" Jessup said as he watched her roll the bike out of the door.

As she stepped out onto the stoop, she immediately regretted not buttoning up her coat. Leaning the bike against the door, she quickly did so and wrapped her scarf around her neck. She placed the bike on her shoulder and carried it downstairs. The sidewalk glittered like glass in the sunlight. *Best to walk it to the office,* she thought. *I don't want to end up in the snow again.*

It took longer than expected and she was a little late. The office was empty as she entered and parked the bike inside the door. When she didn't see Ethan at his desk, she called, "Ethan, are you here?"

"Yes, I'm in Mr. Pennington's office. Just a moment," he called back.

"Okay," she said and started unwrapping her scarf and unbuttoning her coat.

He came out carrying several files. "Why are you in the office today? Did you have something to work on?"

"No. I'm working on your case and wanted to review some details with you."

He immediately perked up and then frowned. "I can't meet right now, I'm due in court for the probate on Dad's will." He glanced down at his watch. "In about twenty minutes."

"I was hoping I could come with you to observe?" She knew probate of the will meant the document is judged to be genuine. It also allowed heirs to manage the property or money left to them as they liked.

"Sure, the company will be nice," he said, getting his files organized to go over to the courthouse. He walked past her to get his heavy coat and hat. Once he was buttoned up, he slipped on his hat and turned to her. "Ready?"

She buttoned her coat back up, wrapped her scarf around her neck, and added her hat. "Yes. Is it ok if I leave the bike here?"

"Yes, we can come back after and discuss my case," he suggested.

They headed out, and Ethan locked the door behind them.

"Don't you need Mr. Pennington to be in court with you?" Emma inquired.

"No, I've assisted him in a large number of these and reviewed them with him. He approved me going alone."

They walked carefully on the icy sidewalks and made their way to the courthouse. Once there, they continued to the specific court that dealt with wills and probate. When they entered, they saw several people waiting in the room for the judge to begin.

"How does this work?" Emma asked in a low voice.

Ethan replied in the same tone. "We'll wait until we're called, then approach the bench to speak with the judge."

"Okay," she said, sitting back in the chair. They waited and watched as other wills were probated. Simple ones were signed off immediately. One that was contested was scheduled for another day.

"What does that mean?" she asked Ethan in a low voice.

"We're here to confirm that the will is genuine. If someone disagrees with any part and they can prove it, the probate may stop until more evidence is produced," he murmured.

She continued to watch the proceedings. The lawyer for the family spoke in a low voice to his clients. She could see they were visibly agitated. *Wills can be an emotional business,* she thought.

After a long wait, it was finally Ethan's turn. He stood and approached the bench. He waved at Emma to follow him up. She moved to stand slightly behind him, her gaze on the judge. He had a copy of the will in front of him.

"This would be an easy case, Mr. Worthington," he said. "All seems in order."

He moved to approve the probate when an officer of the court walked up to the judge and whispered in his ear, handing him a piece of paper.

"Oh, okay," the judge commented as he read it. He looked out to Ethan. "We will not be able to probate this will today. It seems we've received a note that another party wishes to contest it, and they'll be arriving after Christmas. A caveat has been filed to allow the persons contesting the will to have a hearing. We'll hear testimony from you and the person contesting at that time. You'll be allowed witnesses who may testify on your behalf."

"Judge, who's contesting the will?" Ethan asked. He was bewildered at the news. "I'm the only living relative in the family."

He ignored Ethan's first question and went on, "Be that as it may, we'll be looking at The papers provided after Christmas. Until that time, you may not dispose of the property without the court's knowledge."

"Judge, what does that mean? Can I use the house? Maintain it and hire servants?" Ethan asked, confused at this turn of events.

"You may use and maintain the house. Just keep track of the expenses," the judge directed.

"I will, thank you."

He pulled another file for the next case. "See my clerk for an open date."

Ethan knew he had no other options. "Yes, thank you." He took Emma's elbow and escorted her to the clerk's desk in the back of the courtroom.

" Is this normal?" Emma whispered.

"No," he muttered back. "This should've been simple and taken only one court appearance."

"What will you do now?"

"The only thing I can do is meet with the clerk and schedule an appointment."

They walked over to the clerk as the court continued with the next case. While they waited, she turned to him. "Do you know who could be contesting the will?"

He frowned. "No one that I know of. There are no cousins or other living family members."

They waited patiently for the clerk to call them to the desk to schedule their time. When their turn finally came up, Ethan and Emma walked up to the desk.

"Can you disclose who's contesting the will?" Ethan asked the clerk.

"Not at this time," the clerk replied in a bored voice. He got the same question over and over during the day.

Ethan understood there were rules and confirmed the date for his next appearance. He took the paper with the date and told the clerk, "Thank you."

He was silent as they headed back to the office.

"Are you worried?" Emma asked. She was concerned for him.

"A little," he said. "Sometimes people will try to steal the inheritance if they think no one will stop them. I'll have to contact Mr. Pennington and see if he can find out who might be behind this."

She said, "We can still access the house, which is good for the investigation."

"Yes, thank goodness, that's my priority right now."

"Will you have time to return to the office to review the case with me?" Ethan asked.

"Yes, I do have to be at the bakery this afternoon, but I have time now," Emma confirmed.

They got to the office quickly; Ethan had set a brisk pace for them. They stepped in and stomped the snow off onto the rug at the door. They took the time to dust off their coats and hats, before moving to sit at Ethan's desk.

Ethan pulled out paper and a pen. "Let me write a note to Mr. Pennington to ask if he minds if I stop by about the will today."

"Do you want me to run it by his house while I'm out?" she asked as she watched him write it out.

"Would it be too much trouble?"

"No, it shouldn't be an issue."

"I would appreciate it. Thank you." He finished it and gave it to her.

She put it into her pocket for safekeeping and pulled out her notebook. "Ready to discuss my findings?"

He sat back and took a deep breath, "Okay, so what were you able to find out so far?"

"I met with Detective Kelly. He's assigned to the case."

"What case," he said sarcastically.

"Yes exactly." She sat forward and said, "Ethan, all of the evidence does suggest suicide."

Agitated, he stood up. He realized he had nowhere to go and sat back down. "I just don't think he went out of that window alone."

"I agree," she said calmly.

"He just wouldn't do that," he began to argue until he realized what she said. "What?"

"I believe you're right. You know your father and didn't see any signs of depression or behavior that led to this," she said in a reasonable tone.

"Yes." He felt so relieved someone believed him. "If he didn't do it, who did?"

"That's what we have to find out. I think it's related to the weird activities reported at the house."

Ethan leaned his head back on the chair. "I thought I was going crazy. Talking about ghosts killing my father."

"No, you just knew him. I still need to investigate and get our ghost before Christmas," she teased.

"So, what next?" he asked, ready to help.

She continued to study her notes. "I want to interview the doctor."

"Why?"

"The pictures of your father showed that he tried to use his hands and arms to break his fall. I would expect a person jumping, trying to kill himself, wouldn't do that."

"The pictures showed that?" he asked. He wanted reassurance that his father had tried to save himself.

"Yes. His wrists and arms were clearly broken," she confirmed.

He thought about that. "You're going to follow up with his doctor?"

"I am, just to get his opinion, so I can document it for you. Are you still all right with me speaking to him?"

"Yes, of course."

"The servants, do you have an address for them? The ones who got scared and ran off."

"I have the address for the agency we used. You should be able to get all the names and addresses from them. I'll write it down for you." He handed her the information. "When we couldn't keep people, we started using places that could send us replacements as we needed them. They have a good reputation for placing honest people. It was important because we weren't always living there."

"That makes sense," she said. "We have similar positions within our temporary business." She went back to her notes. "The housekeeper and her son are still there?"

"Yes," he confirmed.

"Why weren't they scared away?" she asked curiously.

"I don't know, you'll have to speak with them. I can send them a note today."

"I would appreciate that. Detective Kelly said they were away when your father died."

"Yes, they were out for the entire evening."

Emma thought about that and said, "I'll head to the agency,

Mr. Pennington's, and the doctor's office before I go to the bakery."

"Thanks, Emma."

She smiled as she gathered her gear and her bike to head out into the cold day.

CHAPTER 8

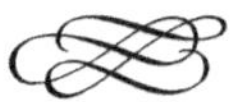

THE KITCHEN AT ETHAN'S FAMILY HOME

A knock was heard at the door.

"Who could that be?" Hannah Shephard asked her son Julian. He sat reading the paper at the kitchen table.

"I'll go find out," he said, as he laid his paper down and stood to walk to the door.

A few moments later, the door swished open as he returned. "Who was it?" his mother asked from the stove. Her soup was starting to simmer and needed to be watched.

Julian was holding a telegram. Reading it, he said, "It's from Ethan. He has an investigator, Emma Evans, looking into his father's death."

Her frown was instantaneous. "Is she coming here?"

His face mirrored hers. "Yes. What will we do?"

A hand moved the vent closed, cutting off their conversation. He sat back and smiled widely. "I know what I'll do. This is going to be such fun!"

CHAPTER 9

Emma wanted to get Ethan's note over to Mr. Pennington first. It was important to her friend. Mr. Pennington lived in a neighborhood very similar to the one in which she lived.

He answered the door on her first knock.

"Emma! What a surprise. Please, come in."

She entered the mostly quiet house. Mr. Pennington was a bachelor and he would be joining extended family closer to Christmas. He led her into his study and motioned to a chair as he sat behind his desk.

"What can I do for you?"

Emma sat and handed over the note. She explained what happened in court with Ethan.

He sat back. "This was not expected."

"Will you look into it?"

"I'll see what I can do."

"Thank you."

"Thank you for helping Ethan."

Mr. Pennington escorted Emma out. She turned to him and

said, "I'm not sure how, but this might be wrapped up with Ethan's father's death."

"Understood," he said. He was aware of how her investigations worked. "I'll let you know what I find out."

CHAPTER 10

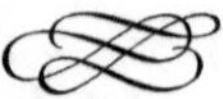

The next address on her list was about four blocks away. She checked her watch, confirming she had another couple of hours before she had to be at the bakery.

She tried to pedal faster as she noticed the snow picking up. The tires crunched on the ice as she pulled to a stop. Not wanting to skid on the wet sidewalk, she got off and carefully walked the bike the rest of the way.

The sign on the door said, 'Personnel Services.' She entered the office and a man was sitting at the main desk in the middle of the room. It was very quiet and had the air of a library. She placed her bike by the door and quietly made her way to him. "Sir?" she asked.

The man looked toward her, disdain clear on his face. He looked pointedly at the water she'd tracked in. "Yes? Do you plan to stand there and get my floor wet all day?"

"No, of course not." Emma looked around for something to clean up the water with.

He just shook his head in exasperation. "What are you here for, young lady?"

"I'm looking into a death that occurred at a house you staffed with servants."

He looked at her curiously. "Is this about the Worthington house?"

"Yes."

"We've decided to terminate that contract. We're not going to send any more servants to that house."

"Why is that?"

"We are getting reports of odd occurrences."

"What kind of odd occurrences?"

"The servants are saying the house is haunted."

"You can't tell me you believe in haunted houses," she scoffed.

Even though he was sitting down, Emma got the impression the man was looking down his nose at her. "No, young lady, we do not, but we do believe that our employees are scared of something, and we can't in good conscience keep sending people over there to be frightened."

"The owner's son has asked me to speak with the prior servants to figure out why they were scared and get it resolved."

He frowned at the girl. "You're looking into it? Shouldn't someone else be doing that?"

He means a man, thought Emma. "No, I'm the one he wants to look into it. Wouldn't it be beneficial for all of us if we can figure this out and have more opportunities for servants to work?"

"Yes," he said begrudgingly. "Well, get on with it, what do you want?"

"I'd like to speak with the last group that worked there."

"We can do that, it isn't a secret," he said as he looked into his card file and pulled out several cards. He looked at her expectantly. "Do you have paper?"

"I do." Emma pulled her notebook out of her pocket.

"Brook Stevens, Beth Arnold, and Margaret Troy," he stated.

"Do you have the addresses where they currently work?" she asked, looking at him.

"I do, but I don't want you jeopardizing those positions," he cautioned.

"I won't," she promised. He read the address to her.

As Emma looked at them, she noticed all three were working at different homes. *This may take a few days,* she thought. She thanked him and made her way back out. His voice followed her out, "Get someone to clean up the water mess!" Grimacing, she regretted that she'd made more work for someone.

Taking her bike, she pulled open the door and stepped out. The wind pushed her back against the closed door and she huddled into her coat as she struggled to walk down the stoop. The weather seemed to be getting worse, but there was one more stop she wanted to make before heading home for lunch. *The doctor.* The pictures were in her bag, and she had questions that needed answers.

His office was located about six blocks away from her current position in the Mann building. The energy it took to pedal the bike made the blocks feel longer than they were. She was breathing heavily when she finally arrived at her destination. Letting out a sigh of relief, she entered the lobby. A guard spotted her and waved her over to his desk.

"Can I leave this with you?" she asked, indicating her bike.

He looked at it, then back at her. "Yes. Will you be long?"

"I don't think so. I'm going to see Doctor Warner."

He nodded. "His office is 225. You can take the stairs up."

"Thank you," she said as she moved the bike to the wall behind his desk. The doorway to the stairs was visible from her location. She went directly there and up to the second floor.

The outer office was quiet when she entered. There didn't appear to be any staff present.

"Doctor Warner?" she called.

A voice called out, "We're closed presently. You'll need to come back at another time."

She followed the voice and found a man reading papers at his desk. "Doctor Warner?"

"I'm Doctor Warner," the man answered, rather impatiently.

"Would you have a moment for me? I'm Emma Evans, and I'm here about Louis Worthington."

Dr. Warner's expression changed at the mention of Worthington's name. "What would you like to discuss, young lady?"

"I'm investigating the death at Ethan's request. I wanted to review the pictures from the scene with you."

"I have some time. Do you have them with you?"

"I do."

"Hand them over, please."

Emma took the pictures out of her bag and handed them to him. "If this was a suicide, why are the wrists and arms broken? Would he have made a defensive posture like that?" she asked bluntly.

Warner frowned. He had seen the breaks; they were listed in his report. "It is possible that he changed his mind on the way down, or it could be a reflex."

"But, Doctor, couldn't it also show that it might not be suicide?"

"It might," he allowed.

"Can I see the death certificate?" she requested.

He looked over and gave her a long look. "Yes. I've completed it." He reached into a drawer, pulled out a form, and handed it to her.

She read it. "What is Visitation by God?" she asked. "That doesn't indicate suicide."

"No," he said quietly. "That means natural causes. I was trying to spare the family by not documenting suicide." He sat back. "I should have looked closer." He sounded regretful at his quick determination.

"I believe it's possible that someone forced him off of that balcony. I'd like more time to prove that. Can you hold off on filing this paperwork until my investigation is complete?"

"Yes, I can do that." He didn't want to be responsible for giving the wrong information to the family. and perhaps helping a murderer go free.

CHAPTER 11

*L*unch she thought. *It's time to head home.*

The temperature continued to drop, and she pulled her scarf up around her face. The wind pushed against her and made pedaling impossible. The bike would have to be walked home.

Her breath was coming in short gasps, and her energy was drained as she parked her bike by the side of the house. She struggled up the front steps and into the foyer, dropping her outerwear to the floor. The cracking of the fireplace in the dining room called to her; she ran over quickly and stood in front of it with her hands spread. With the feeling slowly returning to them she thought about the interview that morning. *I expected Christmas to be a bit boring this year.*

"Stay over there," called Dora as she entered from the kitchen. "We'll get lunch on the table." She moved to set the table with plates and silverware.

"Thanks," Emma said. She was grateful she wasn't being pulled from the warmth. The bakery job would be casting her out into the cold again soon. She looked around and sniffed. "Are those trees I smell?" she asked excitedly.

"Yes, Tim and Patrick brought them home a little while ago," her sister commented. As Dora watched Emma run out to the foyer to find them, she called, "They're not set up yet."

"That's okay, I just want to see them." The smell drew her in, and she found two in the foyer.

Dora followed her out and stood with her, admiring the trees. "These are for the dining room and foyer. The other one is in the sitting room."

"Perfect," Emma said. "This one is big." She indicated the one on the right.

"That one will stay here," Dora said, looking up at the high ceiling in the area.

"Tim did a good job picking them out."

"Me, too!" yelled Patrick, running up to hug his aunt Emma.

"Yes, you did a great job also," she said and returned his hug.

"Yes, you did," Dora told the boy. "And we'll be decorating them tonight."

"Yay!" Patrick yelled.

"Where's Lottie?" asked Emma.

"Nap. She's lying down in the sitting room."

Emma walked into that room and saw the smaller tree. "Oh, Dora," she whispered. "I like this one the best."

"Me, too. We'll have our Christmas morning in here, together."

"That will be nice. Has Tim gotten down the decorations?"

"Here they are," Tim said from the stairs, his arms full of boxes. "I thought I'd get an early start."

Emma and Dora rushed over to help. They moved them to the corner of the foyer.

"Lunch," Amy said as they set them down. They entered the dining room and saw lunch on the table. They sat down and started passing around the large trays.

Tim looked over at Emma. "Have you found anything out about the haunted house?"

"Some." She told them the updates to the case. "Also, an odd thing happened in court today. Someone is contesting the father's will. Ethan doesn't know who that might be. Mr. Pennington promised to look into it."

"Ethan has no idea who it could be?" asked Dora.

"None. He mentioned the uncle to us when we reviewed the case, but he passed before he was born."

As lunch wrapped up, Emma got her winter gear on and was heading out the front door.

"Emma, are you going to take your bike?" Dora called from the dining room doorway.

"No, the roads are too icy. I was sliding around too much this morning."

Her sister frowned. She was concerned for Emma's safety. "Do you need Tim to see about a carriage?"

"No, I'll be ok," she assured her.

Dora looked worried but knew Emma wouldn't take any chances. She went into the sitting room and found a smiling Lottie sitting up. She grinned at her and asked, "Would you like some lunch?" She nodded and squealed when she picked her up.

Emma walked carefully down the stairs. She carried her bag over her shoulder as she made her way to the bakery. The walk was uneventful; it took her longer than expected, but she made it there for her shift on time.

The door to the bakery flew out of her hand and slammed into the wall again as she entered. One of the bakers ran over to help her push it closed. She fell back against the door. "Thank you."

"Anytime," said Michael and returned to his workstation.

Emma headed to the closet to change into her uniform. As she exited, she went to her station and picked up her list. "Cousin," she called.

Cousin looked up from his baking, "Hey, Emma, good to see you. Any questions about your list?"

"Just one. Can I double this Christmas cookie order and take the extras home?"

"Sure, we have enough ingredients. I'll update our inventory. Is the Christmas party planning underway?" he asked. Cousin knew the cookies she wanted were usually requested for the party.

"Yes," she said and smiled. "We're decorating the trees tonight."

"We can't wait for the party. Chloe is bringing her violin," Cousin said with a grin.

"Wonderful, I'm looking forward to seeing the kids."

Chloe and Cousin had gotten married nearly five years ago and had two little boys who looked just like Cousin. They were very happy.

The ingredients she needed were for anise-flavored German Christmas cookies. She pulled them out and worked steadily, getting the dough made and rolled into balls. They went onto trays and into the oven. For the next steps, she prepped the other trays to go in as those finished. The bakery smelled wonderful, and she let herself think about her mama; baking always brought up pleasant memories of her. The bakery had originally belonged to her.

As the first batch of cookies came out of the oven, she pulled them out to cool while she added the second batch.

Two hours later, all of the cookies were out and cooling. She started putting boxes together and placed the wax paper in each of them. When they were ready to go, she filled three boxes for customers and three boxes for her to take home. *Some for decorations and some to eat*, she thought.

"Cousin, the boxes are ready for delivery," she called, pulling off her apron.

He came over to inspect them. "And three boxes for you to take home?"

"Yes," she confirmed.

"Heading out?" he asked as he looked out the window at the falling snow.

"Yes."

"You're sure it's safe? The weather has gotten progressively worse. The snow is coming down hard."

"I should be okay." *Though*, she thought, *it might be a good idea to wait it out.*

Just as she headed to change her clothes, the back door opened and one of the bakers yelled out, "Close the door!"

She looked over to see who was causing all of the issues. It was Jeremy. She went over quickly and kissed him on the cheek.

"What are you doing here?"

"I thought you might want to take a carriage home."

She leaned into him and nodded gratefully.

"Why don't you get changed. We should leave before the weather gets any worse."

"Okay," she agreed and ran to the closet to change while Jeremy talked to Cousin.

He looked around. "Cousin, you might want to start closing up and getting everyone home."

The other man had been considering that. "You're right. Most of the bakers will be heading out as their orders are complete, which should be soon."

"What about the evening deliveries?" Jeremy asked.

"We have a few. But they should be done by carriage and no walking," Cousin confirmed.

Emma exited the closet dressed in her pants, pulling on her coat. "Jeremy, we'll need to take those boxes home," she said, indicating her workstation.

He nodded and headed over to get them. "What about the others? Will we be stopping for a delivery on the way home?"

"Yes, a quick one. Here's the address," she said, handing it to him.

He slid it into his pocket and looked around at the other

bakers who were putting up their work tools and nodded approvingly. Cousin would make sure they got home safely.

"Ready?" Emma asked, wrapping her scarf around her neck and pulling on her hat.

"Yes."

They carried boxes out to the waiting carriage. They went in first and, while she waited, she put her head down into her coat and tightened her scarf. Jeremy finished adding the boxes and turned to help her into the covered carriage. He had a blanket inside; once they were settled, he called up the additional address to the driver and told him to be on the way.

He pulled her close and murmured into her hair, "Better than walking."

"Yes."

"Carriages from now until this weather clears," he said firmly.

She shivered and settled into him. "Agreed."

They made good time to the drop-off. She climbed down and he handed her the three boxes.

"I'll walk this up," she said.

"Are you sure?"

"Yes. It's just down the way."

She hurried down the alley to the side door and knocked. It was answered by a harried-looking cook.

"Thank goodness these arrived. We have guests and no desserts."

"Well, this should help." Emma showed the cook the boxes she held.

"Put them on the table and be quick about it." The cook waved to two waiters to start putting the cookies on the trays. "On your way," she said to Emma, needing to get on with her party preparations.

Emma smiled slightly as she walked back out the door into

the alley. Jeremy would be waiting and the driver was probably not happy with the additional stop.

It seemed darker and more oppressive after being in the bright kitchen. She hurried toward the end of the alley, eager to get out of the cold. Something stopped her abruptly, cutting her air off. Gasping for breath, she reached up to loosen whatever was wrapped around her neck. The hold was so tight, that she couldn't break it and found herself being pulled further into the dark alley. When the pulling motion stopped, she was able to get a more stable footing. She tried to suck in a breath, black spots beginning to take over her vision.

Emma felt a foot near hers and stomped down. The rope loosened enough for her to turn. Though her vision was still cloudy, Emma could tell the person's build was a man. She balled her fists and started punching the man's face over and over.

The counterattack wasn't what he expected and the rope fell away as he tried to get away from her. She let him back away from her, she ran toward him, her boots hitting him in the stomach, causing him to fall backward and slide down the ice to the far side of the alley. The exercise drained her, she struggled to get air into her throat and bent over, trying to catch a breath. As her vision cleared, she could see his body and ran toward him. Hearing her boots in the snow, he pulled himself up and made a mad dash out and was gone by the time she reached the mouth of the alley.

Shaking, Emma returned to her previous location and saw the rope that had been around her neck; she bent down to pick it up. Clasping it tightly, she made her way back toward the waiting carriage.

Jeremy saw her come out and jumped down to assist her. He called up to the driver and gave the direction to head home.

"No," she stuttered, "we need to head to the police station."

Jeremy couldn't see her face in the dark carriage but knew from her tone something was wrong. "Emma, what happened?"

"We need to get to the police station as soon as possible," she stuttered again.

Jeremy didn't hesitate and called out, "Police station instead, please."

The driver followed the direction and headed to the station.

Emma shivered, but not from the cold, and huddled deeper into Jeremy's arms.

When they arrived, Jeremy helped Emma down.

"Go get you and your horse warm," Jeremy called to the driver. "We'll need you here in about an hour. Come get us at that time."

He nodded and clicked his tongue to move the horse on his way.

Jeremy continued to hold her close as they headed into the station.

Officer Jessup was still at the desk and he called out, "Emma, you're back!"

When she didn't say anything, he was puzzled. That wasn't like her.

Jeremy looked at her clenched hands and saw something in them. He took them and worked to unbend her fingers. He saw she was holding a thin rope.

"What is this?" he asked and tilted her head up toward him. That was when he saw the marks on her neck. He realized immediately what had happened in that alley. A rage swept over him, but he pulled it back and turned to Jessup. "We need to see Chief Marsh on an important matter," he said stiffly.

"Well, he normally..." Jessup started.

"No! Now!" Jeremy said. He would brook no denial.

Jessup realized it must be important, so he called another officer and sent him to get the Chief. Jessup took a long look at the still silent Emma. "Why don't we move you both inside?" he asked.

Jeremy took her arm and moved to follow the officer inside and into an empty interrogation room. It was quiet and there were chairs for them to sit in. He sat her down in one of them and moved to sit in the one next to her. He took her hands in his and kissed them. They waited.

The door slammed open, and Chief Marsh entered the room. He was frowning heavily and a bit out of breath from the run down the stairs. Something important must have happened for Emma to call for him directly. Going to her he pulled a chair and sat it in front of her, He noted her pallor and asked gently, "Emma, do you want to tell me something?"

"Yes." She unclenched her hand for him and, lifting her chin, said, "I thought you might want to see this."

The chief sat back in his chair and then stood up and went to the door. "Dan!"

Officer Jessup looked up.

"Go get Detective Carlson," Marsh continued. "He'll want to be here. And tell Jake we'll need the pictures from the two cases this morning."

Jessup left at a run, heading to Detective Carlson's desk and then to get Jake. Detective Carlson and Jake met at the door at the same moment.

Carlson said, "Go ahead, Jake."

He nodded and entered the room. His expression did not change as he greeted them. "Hello, Emma. Hello, Jeremy."

"Hi, Jake," Jeremy said.

Jake looked at Emma, but she didn't say anything.

Detective Carlson entered behind Jake and stayed silent. He was unsure why he was here and why the chief was in the room.

Chief Marsh turned to her. "Emma, could you tell us what happened?"

She shuddered. "I was at..." She stopped abruptly and looked at Jeremy in horror. "We need to get someone over to that house! Once they start leaving, the help and the party-goers could be hurt!"

Jeremy patted her hand. "Chief, before we go much further, you might want to send officers over to 6753 Stomp Street and alley. There's a large party going on there."

The chief realized they needed to move quickly on this. "Carlson, tell Officer Demetri to step in."

Carlson left and returned with the officer.

"Demetri, I need you to get ten officers and head over to 6753 Stomp Street," the chief said. "Cover the residence and the alley."

Demetri started out and then slowly turned to ask, "What are we looking for?"

"Someone lurking around," Emma supplied. "It's related to the two strangulation cases from this morning."

Demetri understood the importance. "We'll head over now and keep our eyes open." He exited the room, closing the door behind him.

"Now, Emma, I'm taking you on faith, but I need to know exactly what happened," Marsh stressed.

Carlson looked confused but stayed quiet.

She started again." I was in the alley at the house on Stomp Street, delivering some boxes of cookies for the bakery. I started walking back toward the carriage and someone wrapped this rope around my neck. He pulled it tight and twisted it."

"The mark we saw on the two victims this morning. What did you do?" the chief asked. He knew she had self-defense training and could handle herself.

"I turned within the hold and started to pound his face."

"Good girl. Can you describe him?"

"Not in any great detail; the alley was very dark. He was about 5'11" and had a hat or covering pulled over his face."

When Marsh frowned, she explained, "I could feel it as I hit him."

"What happened then?"

"I think I scared him because he ran off." She chuckled suddenly. "He fell trying to get out of there fast."

The men laughed at the picture she painted.

Carlson stepped up to the table. "Emma, did you see Jake's pictures of the two crime scenes?" he asked, indicating the brown envelope Jake was holding.

"Yes, I saw them. Detective Kelly permitted me to view them when I went down to get the Worthington pictures." She looked at Jeremy. "Two women were found at separate scenes strangled this morning."

Jeremy's face turned white. He could have so easily lost her tonight. He held himself together on the outside, though he felt like his insides were shattering.

"Carlson, have you found out anything about the current cases?" the chief asked.

The detective looked down at his notebook. "We have their names, Brooke Stevens and Beth Arnold. They lived in boarding houses located near each other. We were able to determine this during the door-to-door canvassing."

The chief noticed Emma start at the names. He focused his attention on her. "Do you know them?"

Jeremy frowned at her and waited for the answer.

Emma nodded slowly. "I don't know them, but I did plan on interviewing them for my current case."

"Which case is that?" asked the chief.

Jake answered for her. "It's Detective Kelly's case. The Worthington suicide."

The chief frowned at this. "Have you been in contact with Detective Kelly?"

"I have," she confirmed.

"Do you see a link between these cases?"

"Not right now," she admitted, "but I just started investigating. I believe Mr. Worthington didn't voluntarily jump from his balcony."

"Carlson, where are we in your case?" Marsh asked, looking over at him.

"We think it's someone who knew both girls. And Emma's right," the detective said begrudgingly. "They both have identical rope marks, very similar to those on her neck."

"Emma, would you be okay looking at the pictures?" the chief asked.

"I saw them this morning, but I can look at them again to see if I see anything." She waited while Jake laid them out.

Once the pictures were displayed, Jeremy stood up and went to the corner to lay his head against the wall.

"Emma, do you recognize either of these girls?" the chief asked.

She looked carefully; she was able to push down her emotions. "No, I only know them by name. I do know that they just switched from the Worthington household to other locations." The nervous energy she had experienced was gone and she looked at Jeremy and back at chief Marsh. "Can we head home?" she asked.

"Yes, but I'll want to have someone watch your house," Marsh said.

Jeremy straightened. "That won't be necessary. She'll be well protected tonight. I'll also make sure she has company until we find out who is behind this."

Emma didn't say anything. This time, her assigned role was as the victim.

"Okay then," the chief said, "let's get you home. Emma, we'll need to speak with you as the case progresses. Keep both Kelly and Carlson informed of any changes in the Worthington case."

Jake spoke up. "Emma, can I get some pictures of your neck?"

She understood Jake needed to document it. "Yes. Can we do it now?"

"I will go get my camera," he said and left the room.

Emma didn't know why, but she picked up the roped again and was running it through her fingers.

"Emma," the chief said gently. "You'll need to leave that here. It's evidence."

She looked up, startled at the statement. "What? Oh, yes. I wasn't thinking." She dropped it to the table; the chief took custody of it and handed it to Carlson.

Jake must have run to his work area and back because he was already in the doorway holding his camera. "Can we move out into the larger area? We need the light."

"Yes, of course," she said and followed him out.

As Jeremy watched her leave, the chief eyed him. "She saved herself."

"Yes, but she could have died, and she was only twenty feet from me," Jeremy said, his voice strained.

He understood and didn't say anything more until Emma and Jake returned.

She walked through the door, her face ashen, and she appeared to be swaying. Jeremy walked over to her. "Ready to go?" he asked in a soft voice.

"Yes, please," she murmured, leaning on him. "Chief, thank you," Emma said softly.

"We'll find this person," Marsh promised, his voice low and emphatic.

Officer Jessup came in. "Jeremy and Emma, your carriage is waiting for you," he said.

Jeremy took her elbow, escorted her out, and lifted her into the carriage. Once he had them settled, he pulled her to him. "Do you want to talk about it?" he asked.

"I'm not usually taken unawares like that. It scared me," she admitted.

"Yeah, me, too."

They sat quietly, listening to the sound of the carriage wheels crunching the icy snow.

"Do we tell the family?" he asked.

"Yes. But we don't let it spoil the night. I need something to keep my mind occupied."

"We can arrange that."

The carriage stopped at their home and he climbed down. He turned to help her out and paid the driver handsomely.

They carried the cookie boxes and headed up the stoop. Loud voices greeted them as they entered. "Everyone is here," she observed as Jeremy helped her take off her coat. She kept her muffler around her neck. Jeremy took both coats and hung them in the closet.

When he returned to her side, he asked, "Do you want to go in? We can go upstairs."

"No, I'm okay," she said and kissed him on the cheek.

Dora came into the foyer. "We're sitting down to dinner. Come in, come in."

Jeremy looked at Emma and she nodded. They went in and, with all the noise of family, no one noticed that Emma and Jeremy were quieter than normal.

Dinner wrapped up. The family was cheerful and looking forward to decorating for Christmas.

"Okay, let's get cleaned up," Dora started. "Emma, why don't you take off that hot muffler."

Emma looked around at Tim, Dora, Abbey, Papa, Cole, and Savannah. "We need a family meeting," she stated softly, her voice strained

"Of course, we'll all be here for the decorating," Dora said, laughing.

"No, Dora, listen. We need to talk first."

Dora realized her sister was being serious and called for

Amy to come out of the kitchen. "Amy, do you mind cleaning up?" she asked.

"No, of course not," Amy replied. She went back to the kitchen to get Ethyl. They began clearing the table.

"Everyone," Dora said to the group, "Emma would like us in the sitting room to discuss something."

Papa walked over to Emma. "Anything I should be worried about, little girl?"

"Let's go into the sitting room," she said noncommittally.

They went in. Patrick was sitting with Tim and Lottie. Dora walked over and dropped down next to them, taking Lottie into her arms.

Jeremy looked over at Patrick. "Patrick, could you go read one of your books while we talk?"

Patrick looked at his papa. "Can I?" he asked.

"Yes," Tim replied and looked more concerned when the request was made. "I'll call you when we're ready to decorate."

The family watched Patrick leave and Jake entered carrying a plate. He had just arrived home. They were quiet, waiting for Emma to begin the meeting. She started unwrapping her muffler and Dora saw what she had been covering. She rushed over. "What happened!"

Emma went into detail about the events of the evening. The group was stunned. "I don't mean to depress everyone, especially with our Christmas plans tonight."

They all started talking at once. Cole held up his hand to quiet them down.

"What did the police say?" He assumed they'd gone there first.

"We went there after the attack and spoke directly to Chief Marsh," Jeremy said. "We found out two girls were murdered this morning and they had the same markings on their necks."

They were stunned at this news and began talking at once.

Jeremy held up his hands. "Additionally, the murdered girls were also the same ones who ran away from Ethan's house. So far, there's nothing other than their work location to connect them."

The conversation continued and Emma became quieter and her face paler.

Jeremy noticed and caught Dora's eye. He indicated for both of them to go out into the foyer. She nodded and followed as he got up.

Once they were away from the group, Jeremy said, "Dora, Emma would like us to behave as if nothing happened and for the family to enjoy Christmas. Let her deal with this in her own time. Do what you do best: marshal your troops, and get us moving to get Christmas going."

She looked over his shoulder at Emma and came to a decision. "Yes, you're right." She walked back into the sitting room. "It's time for Christmas decorations, and we're going to get organized now."

Everyone was surprised by this announcement.

"Tim," she directed, "you and Jeremy get the boxes marked sitting room and we'll do this tree first."

"Savannah and Abbey, could you get the cookie trays and the popcorn? Papa and Cole, help move the drinks in here for us. Patrick," she called down the hallway, "get the popcorn and string from Amy."

Everyone fell into line and moved to their tasks. It gave Dora a chance to go sit by Emma. "When you're ready to talk, let me know."

"I will," Emma said as she wiped a tear off her cheek. Dora pulled her close and sat while everyone got organized. When everyone was back from their assigned task, Dora again took control.

"Okay, get the boxes opened, and let's start decorating!"

While the decorations were sorted, the popcorn and candy

were waiting to be strung, and the cookies and drinks were set up on the table.

"Who wants to add the first decoration?" Tim asked from his location at the tree. He was holding a box of glass ornaments.

"Me, me!" Patrick shouted and ran over. Tim bent down to lift him onto his shoulder. Patrick placed the ornament and clapped. Everyone looked happy at that moment.

Patrick and Tim moved to sit on the floor near Dora and Emma. Amy brought in the large bowls of popped corn and candy. Dora reached behind her, pulled out the string, and handed it and the popcorn and candy over to Patrick to work on. Papa and Abbey were placing the garland on everything from tables to doorways, to the long staircase, and into the dining room. Dora pulled Emma up and joined Jeremy at the tree to add decorations.

Emma smiled for the first time that evening. She turned to Dora. "Thanks for this." She and Dora hugged.

They hung boxes of decorations and used ribbon to add the cookies to the tree. Once the decorations were up, they sat eating cookies and drinking hot chocolate.

Dora leaned over to her sister. "I think we all needed this." She paused and asked, "Will you be able to sleep tonight?"

"I don't know," Emma confessed.

"Try?" Dora asked. "Why don't you go up and have a nice hot bath and relax," she suggested.

"I'm going to take that advice."

Emma set her cup down, stood up, and kissed her sister on the cheek, then went over to Jeremy to whisper in his ear. He nodded. She told the others good night and headed upstairs. The group watched her go.

Cole looked at Jeremy. "Do you think she was targeted based on the current case?"

Jeremy considered that. "If not, the timing is coincidental."

"Nothing seems to link them?"

"Nothing stands out right now."

"What can we do?" Papa asked.

"Nothing. The police are looking into this. We just have to be here for her and the other ladies in our lives."

"Agreed."

The evening wore down and Jeremy made his way upstairs. He entered his bedroom and quickly made his way to Emma's through the secret door hidden by the bookcase. She was coming into the bedroom door with her hair wrapped in a towel and wearing a robe.

"Better?" he asked.

"Yes, much," she admitted.

He walked over to the fireplace and started the fire. It took a few minutes to get the flames going. "Come over here," he called. Taking her brush, she went to sit with him. He held out his hand and she passed it to him.

The room was silent, the only sounds were the cracking of the fireplace. The brushing soothed her and she was having trouble keeping her eyes open. Feeling herself drifting off, she didn't object when Jeremy moved her to the bed. The sheets were cool as he slid her into them and pulled the cover over her. He left to get ready for bed. When he finished, he entered the room quietly, climbed in, and pulled her close. "Mmm," she murmured but did not wake up.

A few hours later, her jerking movements and moans woke him.

"Emma! Wake up! You're okay."

She woke quickly and sat up taking deep breaths. *Home*, she thought. *I am home*. And sank back into Jeremy's arms.

"What were you dreaming about?" he asked quietly.

"It was Zeke. In my dream, he was the man who had me by the neck."

Zeke Jones had beaten and nearly killed her when she was

ten. When he came after her a final time, they were finally able to stop him.

"He can't come back; we've gotten rid of him," Jeremy said, the satisfaction evident in his voice.

"Yes, I know, but my dreams don't," she muttered into his chest.

"Do you want to talk some?"

"I do," she admitted.

"Do you think this is somehow related to the haunted house case?" he asked.

"I do find it suspicious that Ethan's father died under questionable circumstances and then two servant girls who worked for him were found murdered."

"Do you want to stop working the case?"

"Because of this?" she asked, touching her neck. "No, we just have to move forward on our case and trust the police to investigate theirs."

Jeremy believed the two were related but understood this was her decision. "Where do we go next on the case?" he asked.

"There is the one cook I've yet to talk to. I plan on seeing her tomorrow."

"Emma," he said, his voice deepening, "you can't be by yourself until we find out who is behind this."

She chuckled suddenly and asked, "I assume you think I'll argue?"

"Well, yes."

"No, in this case, I'm not going to," she said, touching her neck again. "Could you set up a Pinkerton man to be around?"

"It's close to Christmas, so I think I can take some time and tag along after you. That is, if you'll have me."

"That I will," she said and lifted her head to kiss him. After that, they fell into a deep sleep.

CHAPTER 12

"Good morning." Jeremy leaned over to kiss Emma when they awoke.

"Good morning," she said, stretching.

He moved to the side of the bed and looked back at her. She hadn't made a move to get up. "Are you feeling okay?"

"I'm just taking a moment," she said before she sat up and scooted to the end of the bed.

"How's your neck?"

"Sore," she said, rubbing it.

Jeremy looked over at her but didn't comment. Instead, he stood and walked through the opening behind the bookcase to his room. They got ready and exited their rooms to the hallway. He held out his hand to her. Taking it, she smiled softly as they made their way downstairs.

Breakfast was the normal noisy affair. After they helped clean up, she looked at Amy. "Have you got some time to talk with us?" she asked.

"After I clean up. what can I do for you?" the cook asked as she carried trays back to the kitchen.

Jeremy and Emma followed her in with glasses and plates. "We're working on another case you might help with."

"And you have some servants you need to locate."

"Exactly. But I have to get to the bakery, so would you mind looking at the names and addresses now?"

"Sure," Amy said as she pulled out a chair and sat down.

Jake sat at the table reading his photography book. He had a little time before going to work. Besides, he liked to spend his morning with Ethyl.

"Ethyl, I'll be right with you," Amy told the other girl.

Ethyl smiled, understanding that Amy helped with Emma's cases occasionally. She continued to wash up as the others talked.

"Did you hear about the two maids who were murdered?" Emma asked the two women. Both Ethyl and Amy nodded. "They were two of the girls I was going to ask about, but for now, I need to know about the cook, Margaret Troy," said Emma.

"Yes, I know her," Amy stated. "She should be easy to speak with. But remember what time of the year it is. They'll be quite busy with the season in full swing."

"I will," Emma promised. "What I need is a letter of introduction."

"I can do that. Do you need her work address?"

"No, I got it from the employment agency."

Emma looked at Jeremy, "Would you like to go with me?"

"Just try to stop me."

"I'll write a note for you now," Amy said. She quickly wrote a letter of introduction to explain who Emma was and what she needed. As she handed it to her, she said, "The two girls who died didn't deserve what happened to them."

Jeremy said, "Amy and Ethyl, do not go home without an escort."

"Tim told us this morning, he said he would take care of it," replied Amy and Ethyl nodded.

"Good," he said.

Emma nodded and said, "Thank you."

She took the note, and she and Jeremy left the kitchen.

CHAPTER 13

The two of them reviewed the address together in the foyer.

"It's just a few blocks from here," Emma commented.

"Yes." Jeremy glanced out of the front window. "The sleet has stopped, and the wind has died down. We should be okay to walk."

They gathered up their winter clothes and headed to the first address. When they arrived, Emma looked around. "It's very similar to our neighborhood-working-class, but doing well." The houses were neat and clean, and the sidewalks were cleared of snow.

They arrived at the address and Emma looked around to find the back door. Owners didn't want visitors seeing their servants for personal business. She found it to the left of the building. "This way." Jeremy followed her to the door and stood back as she knocked.

It was only a few moments before it opened to reveal a small woman with her hair pulled tightly into a bun. She had a pleasant expression on her face. "Hello, dear, what can I do for you?" she asked.

"Would you mind if we came in to ask you a few questions?" Emma asked, hoping they could come in from the cold.

"Questions, deary?"

"Yes."

The woman gave them a considering look and finally relented. She stepped back and said, "Please, come in."

They went in and sat down at the table. Each slipped off their hats and scarves. Emma pulled out her notebook and asked, "Are you Margaret Troy?"

"I am," the woman answered cautiously.

"I have this note from my housekeeper, Amy Brown, that helps explain what I need."

Margaret took the note and opened it to read it. She looked a little more guarded but said, "Amy recommends you, so I can take some time. Would you both like some hot tea?"

"That would be wonderful," Emma answered for her and Jeremy.

The housekeeper walked over and filled the kettle, put it on the fire, and then walked back to the table to wait for it to heat up.

"Okay, what is this about?"

"The Worthington's house. You worked there?" Emma asked.

"Not for long," Margaret replied with a shiver.

"Why the short-term position? They need long-term help," Emma observed.

"I really don't want to get into that."

"Can you tell me about Mr. Worthington?" Emma asked, trying to get the woman to open up.

"The job was good and the gentleman a nice enough sort. He needed a lot of cleaning done in a short period of time. We were working very hard on that house. The previous help hadn't done much. And that woman..." Margaret said, her voice trailing off.

"Woman?" Emma asked.

"Yes, Hannah Shephard, she's a manager of sorts. Though I never saw her do much."

Emma knew she had to tread carefully with her next question. "I understood there were some strange things going on in that house?"

"Yes," Margaret said, not sharing any more information.

"Can you tell me about the strange things?" Emma probed.

That seemed to agitate the woman. "I really don't want to talk about it."

Emma pressed, knowing their time was limited. "Did you ever clean Mr. Worthington's room?"

"I think it's time you both left," Margaret said as she stood up with a jerky movement, overturning her chair.

Emma and Jeremy remained seated.

"Margaret, I'm just trying to help Ethan figure out what happened to his father," Emma stressed.

"Please, you need to leave."

"One more thing," interrupted Jeremy. "The two young maids you worked with have been found strangled. Do not leave the house by yourself. Make sure you're accompanied."

This information increased Margaret's agitation; she walked to the door and yanked it open.

"I think you should leave now," she demanded.

"Okay," Emma finally acquiesced. "We'll go, but if you need to talk, this is my address." She tore out a paper with her address and held it out to her.

Margaret took it without saying anything else.

The tea kettle started to whistle loudly.

Emma glanced at the screaming kettle. "Maybe we'll have tea together next time."

They left by the kitchen door. Jeremy hailed a carriage and took her to the bakery for work. Once he walked her in, he turned to her. "Don't leave without me. I'll be back for you."

"I'll wait," she promised.

CHAPTER 14

Jeremy picked Emma up after her shift, and the carriage took them straight home. They sat close, enjoying their time together. Once they arrived home, he helped her down and escorted her to the stoop. A person stepped out of the shadows. Emma took a step back and hit Jeremy. "What?" he said as he stumbled into her.

"Someone's here."

Jeremy looked to see who it was. The person stepped forward, the moonlight illuminating her face.

"Oh, Margaret? Is that you?" Emma asked in relief. It was the cook that they spoke to earlier that day.

"Yes," the woman said in a low voice.

"Why didn't you go in? Amy wouldn't mind," Emma suggested, shivering in the cold.

"I wanted to see you without people knowing," Margaret said, rubbing her hands together. They were in gloves, but they must have been bothering her.

"Would you like to come in?" Whatever she wanted, Emma needed some warmth.

"Yes, that would be nice, but not through the kitchen."

"No, we can go through the front, and you can keep your scarf over your face," said Emma.

"Thank you," Margaret said gratefully.

She followed Emma and Jeremy into the house. Emma waved to the group in the sitting room as they walked by and indicated they shouldn't follow. They entered the study and pulled the doors shut behind them. Jeremy walked to the fireplace to stoke the fire and removed his outer gear.

Emma removed her coat and hat and looked over at Margaret. "Please, take off your coat."

She hesitated, not wanting to stay longer than absolutely necessary. Finally, she took off her gloves and unbuttoned her heavy coat. She handed it to Emma and sat down near the fireplace, warming her hands.

"Margaret," Emma prompted, wanting to start the conversation. Jeremy stood by Emma's chair, silent and observant.

Margaret started where the other conversation had left off. "Yes, I was assigned to clean Mr. Worthington's room."

"Wasn't that unusual? Weren't you the cook?"

"Yes. Well, that housekeeper said everyone had to help out. There were no other family members to cook for except for Mr. Worthington or Ethan who were only expected occasionally, so I was told I had to do other things to occupy my time."

Emma nodded and continued with her questions. "Can you tell me about it?"

"Yes. I went in and pulled the curtains open. They were so dusty; the room hadn't been thoroughly cleaned. I knew I would be in there for a while."

"What happened?" Emma asked, knowing something must have.

"I had been in the room for an hour or more. I had the door closed to the hallway and saw something out of the corner of my eye."

"What was it?" Emma asked, sitting forward.

Margaret hesitated again. "I'm not sure, but at the time, I thought it was a ghost."

"What exactly did you see?"

"Something white flying at me."

"Was it a physical sensation? Did it touch you?"

"No, I don't think so. I ran out as fast as I could, but it seemed to follow me down the stairs."

"It followed you?" Jeremy asked.

"I thought it did. I ran outside and stood there for a long time. I was dizzy from the experience."

"Did you go back into the house?" Emma asked.

"Yes, but I refused to go back to that room."

"When was this?" Jeremy asked.

"The night before Mr. Worthington died. I was expecting him to be there the next evening. Mrs. Shephard finished the room, opening the windows to air it out. The room was very clean at that point."

"What happened when Mr. Worthington arrived?" Emma asked.

"He took his bags up and closed the windows. Everything was quiet."

"What happened next?"

"I didn't wait around. The two other girls and I had a plan. We left," she admitted.

"Why did they want to leave?" Emma asked.

"They had reported seeing strange things in that room. The housekeeper just said they were lazy and were telling stories. "

"But you knew that wasn't true."

"Yes, I had seen the ghost for myself," the other woman said quietly, looking down.

"I understand," Emma murmured. Seeing something like that would make anyone question staying there.

"Miss, do you think it was really a ghost we saw?" she asked, wanting the answer to be no.

Emma didn't want to discount her experience and said, "I don't think so, but I do think something is going on."

Margaret looked relieved that her statements weren't being disregarded.

"I will continue to investigate," Emma promised. "Margaret, did you know the two girls…"

"Were murdered?" she finished for her. "Yes. I knew before you mentioned it this morning. All the maids and cooks talk. They were nice girls, just young and excitable. Do you think this is related to the house? Am I in danger?" Margaret's agitation increased.

"I don't know if these events are connected. Right now, they're being treated as two separate cases," Emma said, trying to calm the other woman down.

Margaret nodded and wiped a tear off her face before looking up at Emma. "Could you let me know if you find out what happened to me at the house? I'll feel more settled if I know."

"I'll strive to do just that," Emma assured her.

They stood and walked Margret to the front door. As Emma watched her put on her coat and wrap her scarf around her face and hair, she said, "One more thing. I would like to send someone home with you."

"I'll do it," Jeremy volunteered. "I'll eat when I return."

"Thank you," Margaret said gratefully.

Emma and Jeremy escorted her to the foyer. Emma watched him put on his coat. "Be safe," she said.

He smiled. "Always." He kissed Emma and then took Margaret's elbow and went out into the cold night.

Time for dinner, she thought. She went into the dining room; it was still ongoing.

Dora fixed a plate for her and handed it to Emma. "Long day?" she asked.

"Very busy. Jeremy is going to take someone home. He'll be

back soon."

"Anything you can share?" Tim asked.

She looked around and saw people she could trust. Tim, Dora, Jake, and Savannah. She was about to start explaining when Jeremy joined them.

"That was quick," Emma observed, watching him sit. He kissed her hello and rubbed his cold nose on hers. She shivered at the contact.

"She only lives a street over from us," he said.

Dora looked at Emma. "Did you get any more information on Ethan's case?" she asked.

Emma covered the information she had compiled that day. "I've been thinking of ways to disprove the suicide. We have the fact his arms are marked from a defensive manner and the distance he was found from the balcony."

"How far?" Tim asked.

Jake answered for her. "Ten feet."

"Ten? That would mean he had to have a running start."

"Yes," Emma confirmed. "That's what I think also. I think whoever or whatever was in the room caused him to run and jump off the balcony."

"And…" encouraged Jeremy. He knew she had a plan as he watched her drum her fingers on her lips.

"Something is happening in that house. I need to continue my inquiries but, eventually, I will need to go there and spend the night."

The group went quiet, and Jeremy said musingly, "So, at Christmas, we're going to stay in a haunted house and wait for a ghost to appear?"

Dora chimed in. "I know who it is! Marley's Ghost!" she said, referencing their favorite book, *A Christmas Carol*.

"Well, it would be fun to speak to four ghosts, but I only need to find out who the one is. Unless one of you requires redemption," Emma teased the group.

They looked at each other and laughed. "Count me in. Sounds fun," Jeremy said.

Dora and Tim looked at the kids, then at each other. Dora answered for them. "We'll stay here and prepare for Christmas."

Jake was quiet, sitting there with his book. Emma motioned to Dora to tap Jake's shoulder. When he looked up, Emma asked, "Jake, what about you?"

"I don't think I could take pictures of a spirit; it would go too fast," he said, his tone serious.

"No doubt," said Emma, wiping her smile off of her face with her hand.

Looking worried, Jake commented, "We still believe that this can be explained through scientific means?"

Emma nodded. "Yes, Jake."

He looked torn and finally said, "I will go. But I want to share a room."

"I think we can arrange that," Jeremy told him.

"We should let Cole, Papa, and Abbey know in case they want to be included," Dora said.

Emma sent Ethan a note and told him she would like to go to the house on Friday. The plan was to spend the night and experience whatever Ethan's father had.

CHAPTER 15

"Ma, they're coming here," Julian said, running into the kitchen. He had another telegram in his hands.

"Who?" his mother asked. She didn't pause her sweeping.

"Ethan's investigators. They're coming here to stay the night!"

That stopped her. She frowned. "Let me see that." She held out her hand for the telegram.

He gave it to her. "What will we do?" he asked, waiting for her response.

She looked at him. "They won't make it through the night."

Julian nodded slowly, waiting for her direction.

CHAPTER 16

The group got organized for the trip. Notes were sent to Ethan, Papa, Abbey, and Cole. Replies were returned confirming that everyone would be at the Worthington mansion the next evening.

Emma and Jeremy checked in with Detective Carlson and found out there had been no more attacks since Emma's. The case had not progressed, and they had no person of interest at this time.

The next evening, the family stood outside the mansion. It was still cold, and their teeth chattered as they made their way up the imposing steps. "A little spooky," Jeremy murmured in Emma's ear.

She shivered from what she hoped was the cold and nodded. The building had something dark about it; the bad weather contributed to the overall feeling.

"Well, it has the look of a haunted house," Cole said, looking around.

"It's the Gothic architecture," Papa confirmed. He pointed out the arches, with peaked windows and diamond-shaped panes.

"It looks like a miniature castle," Jake said.

"It is that," Emma agreed, looking around.

Jeremy walked to the side of the house, frowned, and made his way back. "It appears that it has been added onto over time. The brick appears to start and stop in different color patterns."

"Shall we head up the stairs?" Emma asked.

Each nodded and they walked to the door. As they got close, Emma thought she saw something. She raised her hand and stopped suddenly. "Is that a face?" she asked, looking at the door knocker.

"What's the matter?" Papa asked.

Jeremy leaned in and recognized what it was. There was indeed a face molded into the door knocker. "Why, Marley old man, we were expecting you," he said with a laugh.

"Oh, you. I wonder what else we will see," she commented, raising the knocker and slamming it down with a resounding bang.

The door opened with a creak, adding further to the haunted atmosphere. A shadowy figure opened the door. It was Ethan. Emma released the breath she hadn't realized she was holding.

Not scared of a haunted house, she thought, laughing at her response.

Ethan looked relieved when he saw them. "Welcome all. Please, come in." He held the heavy door open while they went inside.

The entryway was large and dominated by a staircase. The overall look was dark and moody. Heavy paneling covered the hallways and the floor was covered in a dark tile.

Emma looked around. "Is there anyone else here?" she asked.

"Just Mrs. Shepard and her son. Would you like me to show you to your rooms?" asked Ethan.

"Yes. Please," said Abbey, shaking the snow from her hair and coat.

"This way," he said, walking up the stairs.

They picked up their bags and followed him. He showed each person to their room. When he indicated the rooms for Emma and Jeremy, she held up her hand.

"Ethan, I'd like to stay in your father's room."

Ethan nodded. "This way,"

When Jeremy picked up their bags and started to follow, Emma stopped him. "I'd like to stay in there by myself."

"But why?" he asked, frowning.

"The events only seem to occur when people are alone. I need to see what happens," she explained.

He continued to frown, and she reached up to smooth the lines. "Would it help if you inspected the room with me for any secret openings?"

"Yes," he said begrudgingly, "and I'll be outside the door all night."

"Okay," she agreed softly.

Ethan cleared his throat and guided them to the room. "Here it is."

They looked over at him and headed into the room. "Brr," Emma shivered, "it's cold."

"The windows are open. The housekeeper likes to air out the rooms. Do you want me to close them?"

"No, I'll do that when we come up to bed. I'll start a fire then."

Jeremy started walking around the room, knocking on the walls, and Emma looked under the bed and behind the dresser.

"What are you looking for?" Ethan asked, watching them continue around the room.

"Just ways someone could get into the room."

When they finished, he asked, "Did you find anything?"

"No, and I will be staying in here alone tonight."

Jeremy nodded. He understood this was how she wanted to lead the investigation.

Later, before dinner, they split up to investigate the house. The groups set out in pairs, Jeremy and Emma, Jake and Cole, Abbey and Papa.

Jeremy and Emma headed to the basement.

"Can we get drawings of the house? Do they exist?" Papa asked Ethan.

"No, my great grandfather built it himself. So, there wouldn't be any," Ethan said.

Abbey and Papa used a lantern to look around the attic. "How did we get the dusty area?" she asked disgustedly as she picked up the cloths covering the furniture.

"Yes, but better than the basement," Papa said, noting the pictures stacked against the wall. "There does appear to be other relatives," he said, looking through the pictures.

"EEK!" she screamed.

He chuckled. "Abbey, what is it? A mouse? They won't hurt you." When she didn't answer, he walked over to where he had left her. "Abbey? Where are you?"

A hand wrapped over his mouth and he thought, *That smells funny*. Then all went black.

Jeremy and Emma were assigned the basement. Cole and Jake were assigned the main floor, and Ethan was assigned the bedrooms. They went through each, not finding much.

Jeremy and Emma looked around. There was little to see, but he noticed something by the wall.

"What is it?" she asked.

"Chains," Jeremy said, going over to them. "Well, Mr. Worthington loved the book; he may have used them to scare guests."

"Or someone else is trying to scare him," she suggested.

They continued to look around but found nothing.

"It is getting late," Emma said. "We need to head up and see if the others have found anything." She looked at Jeremy and noticed he was focused on a door. "Did you see something?"

"Did Ethan mention what this door leads to?"

"Yes, he said it was a utility tunnel out to the fountains in the front."

Ethan's voice called from above, "Come up, we have dinner waiting."

Jeremy looked conflicted; he really wanted to try that door.

"We can come back and check it later," she promised.

They headed upstairs and went to the dining room to find Cole, Ethan, and Jake.

"Where are Papa and Abbey?" Emma asked.

"They said they would see you in the morning," Mrs. Shephard said.

Emma frowned. "It seems a little early for them to turn in."

"I'm sure they're fine," commented Cole.

"Dinner is in the kitchen. I'll need help with moving it to the dining room," Mrs. Shephard said.

"We can do that," Emma said. They all went into the kitchen to get the dinner trays. Emma looked around and asked nonchalantly, "I understand you have a son."

"I do," Mrs. Shepard replied, not looking up from the glasses she was filling.

"Is he around?" *And is he the man I beat up a few days ago?* she asked herself.

"Yes, he's outside gathering wood for the fireplaces. You should see him later."

"Hmm," commented Emma. "I'd like to interview you both."

"We'll work something out."

They moved into the dining room and as they began to eat,

Emma turned to Ethan. "Ethan, did you find out who's contesting the will?"

Mrs. Shephard stood as still as a statue waiting for his answer. Ethan didn't notice the woman's response, but Emma did.

"Not yet. Mr. Pennington is trying to find out. It is odd, though; I don't have any close relatives who could contest it."

"You mentioned an uncle?" Jeremy asked.

"Yes, but he's dead."

"Did he have any children?" asked Emma.

"I don't think so. He wasn't married."

"Do you know where he's buried?" she asked, wondering if the man was in fact dead.

"In a small graveyard, way out in the back. Grandfather's there and I'll place Dad near them."

So, probably not the uncle, Emma thought wryly. That brought her back to Mrs. Shephard and her son. *Did they contest the will? And Julian—was he the one who attacked her? Was that how this case was going to close?*

Cole changed the subject. "Your father rather liked Dickens' books?"

"Yes, particularly *A Christmas Carol*."

"We saw chains in the basement," volunteered Jeremy.

Ethan laughed. "Yes, he liked to spook people at Christmas with those. It was all in good fun."

"Are there any other things he added?" Jeremy asked, thinking about the chains and the door knocker.

Ethan thought about that. "No. Not really."

They sat together discussing the house and its various eccentricities.

Finally, Emma yawned. "I'd like to go to bed."

"I'll come up with you," Jeremy suggested.

She nodded and held out her hand to him. He took it and the others watched as they ascended the stairs.

Cole looked around. "I think I'll step outside for a cigar. Want to come with me, Jake?"

"No, I think I will head up also."

He went up the stairs and entered his and Cole's room. Turning the knob, he was thinking of reading his camera book. He took a step in and was grabbed by someone behind the door. He struggled, but something hit him on the head. His limp body was drug out of the room and down the hall.

Cole stepped outside and lit up his cigar. The smoke curled up around him. The night air was cold. Moving further out onto the porch, he looked up at the clear night sky. He took the cigar out of his mouth and a cloth was pulled over his face and his hands bound quickly in ropes. No one noticed the cigar as it fell to the ground.

Emma stepped out of the bathroom in the hall and saw Jeremy sitting in a hard-backed chair. "You couldn't find one that was more comfortable?" she teased.

"I don't want to take a chance that I might fall asleep."

"I'm sure I'll be fine. I don't believe in ghosts. If something is happening here, there is a reasonable explanation." She changed the topic. "What are your suspicions with the will?"

He laughed. "Caught that, did you? Mrs. Shephard seemed to be frozen solid when that came up."

"We haven't seen the son yet."

"You think he was the one who attacked you?"

"I think he might be," she admitted. "They seem to be the only people in Ethan's life who might have a stake in this house."

"We should find him; the bruises will prove it was him."

"Yes, that's what I'm thinking. We can check in the morning," she suggested.

She leaned in to kiss him goodnight and went into her room,

closing the door behind her. "Brr," she said. The windows were still open. No w*ood*, she thought. *First things first.* She went to the gas lamps and turned them up. Next, she closed all the windows, hoping that it would be warmer.

Her bag was nearby and she quickly changed into her night-clothes. Glancing toward the bed she noted the heavy curtains surrounding it. *Another Dickens item*, she thought. In *A Christmas Carol*, Scrooge's maid had pulled the curtains around Scrooge's bed down and sold them after his death during the visions with the Ghost of Christmas Yet to Come.

The thought made her shiver, but she shook it off, grabbed the curtains, and pulled them open. When nothing appeared, she chided herself. "I thought you didn't believe in ghosts." She laughed. She was happy to discover the bed was made with thick blankets. Quickly, she walked to the gas lamps, turned them off, and ran back to the bed. She snuggled down and regretted she didn't have Jeremy next to her. The curtains were closed on two sides but open on the side nearest her. Sleep came quickly.

"What? What was that?" she asked, trying to pull herself out of her dreams. She shook her head trying to clear it.

"*Emma*," a soft voice called. "*Emma, you need to wake up*," it called again.

She frowned in the dark. "*Mama?* No, that can't be right." Though it sounded just like her.

Emma struggled out from under the heavy covers, trying to see where the voice was coming from. There was nothing in the room, and then she felt something brush by her. When she turned toward it, half expecting to see Mary; instead, she was face-to-face with Zeke. She screamed and fell off the bed and onto the floor. "Dead! You're dead!" she screamed again.

Jeremy burst into the room and saw her trembling on the floor. He ran to her and wrapped his arms around her. She was shaking.

"Get me out of here," she said.

He did as she asked and helped her up and walked her to the hallway. He sat her down in his chair and knelt in front of her, rubbing her ice-cold hands. "What happened? What did you see?" he asked.

"Can we go to your room?" she asked. She was scared the ghost would follow them.

"Yes, of course." He brushed back her hands and carried her to his room, setting her on the bed. "Now, tell me," he asked softly as he sat next to her. "Did you see something?"

"First, I heard what sounded like Mama calling me."

Jeremy looked shocked. "Is that what caused you to scream?"

"No. It was Zeke. He was in the room with me."

"Zeke? But, Emma, you know he's dead. He can't hurt you anymore," he reasoned.

"I do know that but, at the time, it seemed real."

"Was it a ghost?" he asked hesitantly.

"You know I don't believe in them. And all my research suggests most hauntings are reported by people either drugged or drunk. Or just someone playing a game. There's also waking dreams and powers of suggestion."

"Well, you certainly weren't drunk or drugged. Were you completely awake?" he asked, trying to follow her reasoning.

"I was asleep, but no, I was awake when I saw Zeke."

"Then what could it have been if that room isn't haunted?" he asked, thinking.

Emma looked around. "Could you hear me scream from out in the hallway?"

Jeremy looked at her seriously. "Yes, scared me so much I almost fell off my chair."

"Then why didn't anyone else come out of their rooms?" she

asked as she exited Jeremy's room and wandered down the hallway.

"I don't know," he said. "They should have."

Emma frowned; this wasn't like her family. She tapped on her Papa and Abbey's door. When there was no response, she knocked louder. She looked over at Jeremy.

"Let's try opening it," he suggested.

"Papa? Abbey?" she called. "It's Emma. I am coming in."

She went in first and returned quickly. "They aren't there! And the beds haven't been slept in."

"What?" He ran into the room.

"I'll try Cole and Jake's room; you check on Ethan," Emma told him.

They separated and Emma heard him call out, "Emma, Ethan's not here!"

She ran over. "Neither are Cole and Jake. Where did they go?"

"Downstairs?" he suggested.

"We have to check."

They ran down into the main living room and looked around.

"Nothing," Jeremy observed.

"Kitchen?" asked Emma.

They ran there—no one. They went through every room on the first floor.

"Where are they?" asked Emma, bewildered.

"Who are you looking for?" a young man's voice called from across the dark room.

Emma stiffened and said, "That's Julian, the son. It has to be."

Jeremy called out, "Come out here where we can see you."

Julian stepped into the light. Emma walked close to him and looked at his face. "No bruises," she observed.

"No, I don't have any bruises," he said, bewildered at her statement.

"Where is everyone?" Emma asked.

"The same place you're about to be," he said and reached out to grab her. He didn't realize what was happening until he was face down on the carpet with his arm twisted behind his back.

"Where is everyone?" Emma demanded. "I'm not going to ask again."

"That is something I would like to know," a voice called from a dark corner of the living room. He lit the lamp in his hands and moved toward them.

Emma started violently. It had to be him, the man who attacked her in the alley. His face was covered with bruises.

He noticed her staring and rubbed his face lightly. "You did a fine job on my face, little girl. You caused me to have to hide, and I couldn't continue my fun."

Jeremy wasn't watching the man's face; he was watching his hands. He had a gun pointed at them.

The man saw Jeremy's interest. "Not my normal choice. I much prefer a rope. But sometimes you have to make do."

"Who are you and what have you done with our family?" Emma asked, her voice devoid of emotion.

"Me? We'll get to that later, little girl. I have the same question, though, and I think that young man there might know."

"You won't find them," Julian said.

Emma looked at Jeremy in confusion. *What is happening here?* she mouthed. Jeremy shrugged. He was as confused as her.

"You think not?" The man laughed at them. He seemed to be enjoying the game.

Emma let go of Julian's arm and let him up. Julian faced the man.

"You won't find them" he repeated. "We will stop you *this* time."

The man didn't answer. He shifted his gun to his left hand and pulled out a piece of rope.

Emma paled when she saw it. She already knew he was the

man who'd attacked her, but the appearance of the rope made her lightheaded. Bracing herself, she was determined that, if she was going to die, she would die fighting.

"Now, for the girl, I'm going to finish what I started in the alley. For you two, it's a bullet. I'll do you first." He pointed the gun at Jeremy.

"Wait!" Jeremy said.

"What is it? I have things to do."

"If I have to die, I want one last hug from Emma. I don't want to die without her knowing how much I love her."

"Oh, very well, but hurry. I have so little time and so many people to kill."

Jeremy opened his arms and Emma walked toward him. As she got closer, Jeremy turned his body slightly so Emma could see something in his belt. She looked hard at the object. It was her knife! Emma hugged Jeremy and, as she did, she grasped the knife handle.

"I love you," she said.

"I know," he replied.

Emma pulled her knife out of the sheath. Jeremy stepped back and she whirled and threw it toward the man. The knife rotated blade over handle until it tore into the man's shoulder. He looked down at the knife embedded into his arm.

"I'll be damned," he said and dropped the gun to the floor

Emma turned to Jeremy. "How did you...? When..."

He gave her a half-grin. "I picked it up before we left the bedroom to search for everyone. I thought it might come in handy."

"Why didn't you give it to me before now?" Emma asked.

"Obviously, there's no place on you to hide it at the moment," he said, looking pointedly at her nightclothes.

"Good point."

"The little girl has teeth. I'll give her that," the man said as he swayed on his feet and pulled the knife from his shoulder. "That hurt. But not as much as I'm going to hurt you." He began to walk toward them with the knife in one hand. "I'm going to enjoy this."

"You missed," Jeremy chided her, noting the man was still a threat.

"I didn't miss."

"Why's he still walking then?"

"I want answers and a dead man can't provide them."

Emma and Jeremy positioned their bodies into fighting stances. If they were going down, they were going down fighting.

Bang!

Emma and Jeremy dropped to the floor. They watched the mysterious man grasp his bloody hand and fall to his knees.

Emma looked at Jeremy. *"Who?"*

Hannah Shephard walked into the room. She was holding a gun and kept it aimed at the man.

"Ma!" Julian ran over to her.

The man she'd shot was writhing on the floor. Jeremy took custody of the gun. Emma stood and walked over to their assailant, taking the knife out of his limp hand. She was tired and wanted some answers.

"Everyone in the dining room, now," she said. Jeremy and Julian moved the wounded man to chair, tying him up. "Mrs. Shephard, I assume you and Julian know where everyone is located?"

"Yes," she said, "we do."

"I'll let everyone out," Julian said.

"Where do you have them?" Jeremy asked.

"Basement room, off to the left."

Jeremy cocked an eyebrow at Emma.

"Yes, fine. I should have let you investigate that room," she said.

He laughed and went down with Julian to bring everyone

up. As they returned, they were all talking excitedly at the same time.

Cole entered first with Jeremy. He looked at Emma. "Got it worked out yet?"

"Almost," said Emma, turning toward the man they had tied up.

Her suspicions were confirmed when Ethan entered and said faintly, "Except for the bruises, he looks just like my father."

"He's your uncle," Emma stated, the one you told us had died.

"Uncle Robert?" Ethan asked, stunned.

Abbey, Papa, and Jake entered next.

"Emma, I would like to go home now," Jake said.

She laughed. "So would I, but first, let's find out what's happening here."

Cole looked at Julian. "Is this the one you told us about?"

"Yes, be careful with him. He's dangerous."

"He doesn't look dangerous to me," Cole said.

Ethan looked at his uncle. "They said you were dead."

Robert winced in pain. "Well, that *was* the agreement. I was to leave and never come back."

"And why was that?" Emma asked.

When he didn't look like he was going to answer, Hannah spoke up. "We were teenagers in the same house. And he started playing his games back then." Hannah pulled back her high-necked blouse, exposing an old rope mark. "He snuck up behind me one night and tried to strangle me. I put up a fight. His father somehow heard us and pulled him off me. I almost didn't survive."

"But there's a grave with your name on it," stuttered Ethan.

"That was our father," Robert said disgustedly. "He wanted to make sure I couldn't come back and claim the house. He wanted your father to have it all."

"Were you responsible for dad's death?" Ethan asked.

"How could I be? Didn't a ghost kill him?" he said mockingly.

Ethan looked confused and turned his gaze on Emma. "I think I can answer that." She had worked it out. The effects she experienced in the bedroom were the same as those when she had been exposed to a gas leak on a construction job. Turning to the group. "The gas lamps in Mr. Worthington's bedroom must be leaking. Not enough to notice, but enough to cause headaches, auditory hallucinations, fatigue, melancholy, and other symptoms if someone stayed in the room for long periods. When did you figure out how to set the gas lamps to leak?"

Robert frowned and looked confused. "What gas leak? I don't know what you're talking about."

"He doesn't, but I do," Hannah admitted.

All eyes turned to her.

"No, Ma! Don't!" Julian begged. He didn't want her confessing.

"But I am responsible," she admitted.

Ethan sat down heavily on a chair at the table. "You? But why did you kill Dad?"

"It was an accident," she said, holding out her hand to her son. He took it. "Julian and I found Robert's hidden crawlspace a few years ago. We've monitored it since that time, waiting for him to come back, hoping he was truly dead. When we found his things there, we knew he was back. We wanted to protect the people in this house. I experienced a gas leak previously and saw the effects and I thought I could control it."

"It worked with the cook and the maids," Emma commented. That must be why the windows were open all the time, even in the cold.

"Not that it helped; he got to them anyway," Hannah said bitterly. "Ethan, I didn't mean to kill your father, only to scare him into remaining in town until after Christmas. That night, Louis was reading *A Christmas Carol* again and drinking some port before returning to his room. The gas leak and the port must have caused him to see something, and Louis ran and jumped off the balcony."

"What was your plan about Robert?" Cole asked.

"With Louis gone, we were going to get rid of Robert, once and for all, so Ethan would never find out," Hannah admitted.

"Why did you take such a personal interest and stay here all of these years?" Emma asked.

Hannah looked down at the hand that held hers.

"It was for me," Julian said.

"Yes, he didn't just strangle me; he forced himself on me. Robert's father stopped him from killing me but not from that. I got Julian." She looked at Ethan and said, "Your father allowed me to stay and raise him here. I did love Louis so much, and I am so sorry he is gone."

Julian and Ethan started to cry at her statement.

"I have a son!" Robert said.

Julian looked at him in disgust. "No, you do not! You are not my father."

That definitive statement seemed to shut him up.

Julian said, "This time, you won't be sent away. You will hang for your murders."

"Just one thing." Emma looked at Robert. "Why did you kill the two housemaids?"

He shrugged. "Seemed like fun and kept me busy until the will was probated."

"You're the one contesting the will!" Ethan exclaimed.

"Yes, it's my house! Not yours!" he shouted. "I came back because it is mine, not some snot-nosed kid! Mine!"

Cole looked at him. "No, sir, it is not your house. Your house will be a cell the rest of your short life."

Robert leaned forward and placed his head on the table.

Ethan walked over to Julian and put an arm on the other

man's shoulder. "No, the house belongs to Julian and me. Hannah and Julian can stay as long as they like."

Julian smiled widely.

Cole looked at Jeremy. "Let's take Robert to the police station. It's time to clean this up."

CHAPTER 17

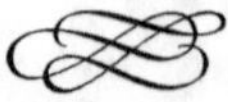

CHRISTMAS EVE PARTY

*E*veryone was dressed in their finest holiday clothes. The house was filled to the rafters with family and friends. Food covered every surface and drinks were delivered by maids. The music was coming from the foyer, Chloe's musical group was playing Christmas music.

Emma and Ethan sat on the couch, watching the room full of people. They were discussing his case.

"Why did your grandfather fake your uncle's death?"

"My theory?" he asked.

Emma nodded.

"He wanted to get Robert away from here. The family name is what he would have been concerned about and he wouldn't have wanted a long, drawn-out trial."

"Do you think he knew he might have continued hurting women?"

He shook his head. "I don't know, but I do know when Grandfather died, he looked drained of life. I think the decision wore on him."

"Will you dig up the grave?"

"No, I don't think so. The police have his statements, so

they'll probably not go to that level."

"Ethan, what form do you think your father's apparition took?" Emma asked curiously.

He smiled slightly. "I think it might have been Marley from *A Christmas Carol.*"

"What makes you say that?"

"When Dad mentioned his brother, he always said he didn't want to be like him, make the same mistakes." Ethan saw something that attracted his attention.

Emma glanced where he was looking and saw his gaze was now on Savannah. She leaned forward and whispered in his ear, "You might take Savanah a drink; she looks thirsty."

He grinned at her. "I'll take one over now." He snagged a glass of eggnog from a server and headed toward her.

Dora dropped down next to Emma. "I'm glad you invited Ethan."

Emma looked at him, talking animatedly to Savannah. "I think Savannah is also."

"What will happen to Mrs. Shephard?"

"Ethan is working with the lawyers to prove it was an accident. We believe she'll be exonerated soon. The judge let her be with Julian for Christmas."

"What will happen to his uncle?"

"Trial. Prison for sure. After that, probably hanging."

"Much deserved," Dora said, thinking of all of those women he had killed.

"I wish there had been a way for different cities to compare cases; we might have caught him sooner," Emma lamented

"That's a future view. We can hope that's something we'll see in our lifetimes."

"Yes."

"Merry Christmas, Emma."

"Merry Christmas, Dora."

RECIPES REFERENCED IN THE BOOK

RECIPES

Anise-flavored German Christmas cookies
Ingredients:

- 4 large eggs
- 2 1/4 cups of confectioners' or super-fine sugar
- 4 cups of flour
- 1 teaspoon of baking powder
- ½ cup of anise seed

Directions:

- Beat eggs until thick. Gradually add sugar and beat well until combined. Fold under the sifted flour and baking powder. Roll out dough to about 1/2 inch thick.
- Flour the Springerle mold each time it is used and press firmly into dough. Remove mold and cut the cookies along the outside lines of the imprint.

- Place cookies on a board or cookie sheet that is sprinkled with anise seeds. Let dry in a cool room overnight. Butter a cookie sheet and place Springerle on it.
- Bake at 250°F until light golden on the bottom and white on top (about 15 minutes).

German Apple cake
Ingredients:

- 3 large eggs
- 2 cups of sugar
- 1 cup of vegetable oil
- 1 teaspoon of vanilla extract
- 2 cups of all-purpose flour
- 2 teaspoons of ground cinnamon
- 1 teaspoon of baking soda
- 1/2 teaspoon of salt
- 4 cups of chopped peeled tart apples
- 3/4 cup of chopped pecans

Frosting:

- 1 package (8 ounces) of cream cheese, softened
- 2 teaspoons of butter, softened
- 2 cups of confectioners' sugar

Directions:

- In a large bowl, beat the eggs, sugar, oil, and vanilla. Combine the flour, cinnamon, baking soda, and salt; add to egg mixture and mix well. Fold in apples and nuts. Pour into a greased 13x9-inch baking dish. Bake at 350°F for 55-60 minutes or until a toothpick inserted in the center comes out clean. Cool on a wire rack.

- In a small bowl, beat cream cheese and butter. Add confectioners' sugar, beating until smooth. Spread over cake. Refrigerate leftovers.

Notebook Mysteries
Kimberly Mullins

ABOUT THE AUTHOR

Kimberly Mullins is the author of series of books titled "Notebook Mysteries". Her stories are based on historical events occurring in 1871-1890's Chicago. She holds a BS in Biology and a MBA in Business. She lives in Texas with her husband and son. When she is not writing she is working as a Process Safety Engineer at a large chemical company. You can connect with her on her website www.kimberlymullinsauthor.com.

Photo Credit: Blessings of Faith Photography

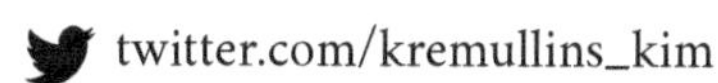 twitter.com/kremullins_kim